SHADOWS OF DANGER

Diana is uneasy when she has a premonition of an air disaster. But when she meets charismatic widower Louis, she is terrified — for he is the man in her dream. Soon she is in love with Louis, but her fear for his safety becomes acute. It seems the only way she can protect him is to marry a man she does not love. Would Louis ever forgive her for leaving him? Would true love eventually win through?

ANGELA DRACUP

SHADOWS OF DANGER

Complete and Unabridged

LINFORD
Leicester

First published in Great Britain in 2012

First Linford Edition
published 2013

British Library CIP Data

Dracup, Angela.
    Shadows of danger. - -
(Linford romance library)
1. Love stories.
2. Large type books.
I. Title II. Series
823.9'14–dc23

ISBN 978–1–4448–1430–9

Published by
F. A. Thorpe (Publishing)
Anstey, Leicestershire

Set by Words & Graphics Ltd.
Anstey, Leicestershire
Printed and bound in Great Britain by
T. J. International Ltd., Padstow, Cornwall

This book is printed on acid-free paper

1

Twenty years ago when Diana was six years old, her mother had taken her to a fortune teller. The woman was old, with deep cracks of skin framing her eyes and fanning downwards to her mouth. She had long, black hair tied in a knotted scarf and gold earrings that twinkled in the dusty light of her little room.

Diana had been fascinated, staring into the crinkled face with its glinting penetrating eyes and sensing its magnetism. And just sufficiently afraid to feel a tiny thrill of excitement.

Her mother had sat with clasped hands, questioning earnestly in her breathless, rushing way. Then gradually she fell silent as the woman looked up from her cloudy glass ball and began to speak.

Long, slow sentences; a ripe, black-treacle voice. Diana had watched the deep red lips move, attending more to the lulling rhythm of the words than their content, which for a child was mainly baffling.

Her mother, however, had listened intently; shoulders hunching, knuckles clenching. At the end of the reading she had rushed from the room, sobbing noisily. A perplexed Diana, trotting in pursuit of her wailing parent, had twisted round for a last glimpse of the strangely magical woman who had the power to conjure up so much noise and grief.

* * *

Louis Rogier stared into the glistening yellow pool at the base of the pan, turning down the gas jet and flicking his wooden spoon at precisely the right moment to promote a rapid thickening, which transformed the small, smooth lake into an opaque, fluffy mound. Another flick transferred this little work of art onto a warmed plate to nestle within a garland of sliced tomatoes and sprigs of parsley.

'Sofia, your egg is ready.'

His daughter was sitting at the table, writing in a small notebook with painstaking care. She closed her book, looked at her plate and smiled. 'Yummy!' She picked up her fork.

'May I take a look at your work?' Louis enquired gently.

Sofia nodded, smiling and pleased.

Louis looked at the childish handwriting: distinctive, bold and primitive. It reminded him of the energetic, mainly incomprehensible, images displayed in Poppy's chic Manhattan gallery. Work produced by supposedly mature adults.

A sharp picture of his ex-wife sprang into his mind. He saw her standing in her chic art gallery, illuminated by a slash of brilliant sunlight from the huge skylight windows, a gilded halo around her blonde head. He closed his eyes briefly, hunched his shoulders against the pain.

Don't think of her, he told himself, aware of an ache like an iron bar in his chest.

He forced his concentration back to Sofia's chunky script. She had written two long strings of words; a column of English nouns on one side of the page, their counterparts in French on the other. He noted that her spelling was accurate in both languages, even though it was only in the last year that Sofia had begun to speak fluently and with confidence. And all because of Poppy, who had been determined that their child should be brought up to be bi-lingual, acquiring the languages of English and French simultaneously.

'After all, darling,' Poppy had told Louis fondly, 'you abandoned your family and your country to be with me. It's the very least I can do to make sure our little one speaks your language like a native.'

She had paused, smiling, her elegant and capable hands clasped around her swollen belly.

'French,' she had declared, 'is the language of chivalry, after all — the language of love.'

An enchanted, infatuated Louis had gazed at his wife in smiling admiration.

'I shall start straight away,' she had declared. 'As soon as the little one is born — talking in both French and English.'

And that was what happened. In the daytime when Louis was working, Poppy talked and sang to her infant constantly. In the morning the baby heard only English, then in the afternoon the stimulating entertainment had been all in French. Poppy's own French was impeccable, as her family had lived in France during her teenage years.

The baby Sofia had watched and listened to her mother with attention and delight. As recognisable words began to emerge, so Poppy would gently correct any crossover between the two languages. But Louis had gradually become uneasy when he noticed the growing anxiety in the baby's huge dark eyes.

He talked to Poppy about it. She was light-hearted and dismissive. 'You wait, darling. In a year's time we shall have a little girl who will be able to hold her own equally well in both London and Paris.'

In a year's time, they had a child who was more or less silent. And it was not until some time after Poppy left that Sofia had begun to make a hesitant re-start in forming words.

Looking now at the words written in her exercise book, Louis felt a surge of tenderness and pride.

'Hey, this is really great stuff, Sofia.' He touched his daughter's soft fringe with tender fingers. 'So, your teacher — Miss Peach — is giving you home-work now, is she?'

Sofia shook her head. 'She says children should play and do what they like when they get home.'

'Is that right?' He raised a quizzical eyebrow. Louis was inclined to agree; the pressure would pile on soon enough.

'I wrote the words because I wanted to,' explained Sofia, taking the book from Louis and stashing it in her zip-up bag.

'Good for you,' Louis said, inclined to agree with Miss Peach's ideas on childhood.

'Yesterday Miss Peach had a bright green shirt and earrings like little parrots,' Sofia mused. 'And she had red heels — very high ones.'

Louis was amused. The exotic-sounding Miss Peach had been a regular feature of conversation in the past months since she had taken on the role of Sofia's language tutor.

Sofia had been receiving special tutoring in English for some time now, ever since her head teacher had called Louis in to express concern at the little girl's reluctance to speak in class.

Louis had been alarmed.

'What do you recommend?' he had asked.

'I suggest that Sofia join in with a small group of children who need some extra help with spoken English.' The head had explained that as they were a multi-cultural school, a tutor visited twice a week to teach English.

'Very well,' Louis had agreed, not wholly convinced. 'Let's give it a try.'

Slowly Sofia began to come out of her shell. And once Miss Peach arrived on the scene, her confidence rocketed. Soon she was able to tell Louis in detail all she had done at school each day — and all about her lovely tutor, Miss Peach.

Louis glanced at his watch. 'Nearly time to be going.'

Sofia put her furry pencil case in her shoulder bag and smiled up at her father. Love and understanding flowed between them.

'Teeth,' she said solemnly.

He heard water running in the bathroom, imagined her brushing vigorously. Such energy she had, such vitality surging with the optimism of childhood.

He had a swift sense of the weight of his own thirty years sitting heavily on him. Dear God! Sometimes he thought he could not have made a greater mess of things if he had deliberately set out to do so.

He heard the rattle of the letter box and grimaced. The arrival of mail rarely brought any joy these days; only bills — and letters from Poppy, which made his eyes wet.

Galloping down the steps Sofia scooped up the envelopes.

'One for Daddy,' she announced, handing Louis a thick cream envelope. 'Two for me!'

She laid her letters on the table. There was a cream envelope identical to the one Louis had received. And a bright pink one addressed in immaculate italic script in vivid purple ink.

'Which one shall I open first?' she mused.

Louis stared at the envelope in his fingers, registering Poppy's dramatic writing, full of swirls. With a flash of insight he knew what it contained. His heart sank as he tore it open.

The card inside was thick and stiff, embossed with raised shiny script. It was an invitation to a wedding to take place in an expensive Manhattan hotel.

A marriage between his former wife and her lover, Liam.

So it was really over — all that he and Poppy had shared.

He glanced at Sofia who was holding an identical card at arm's length, her head cocked in a bird-like pose. Quietly, with great dignity, she turned the card over and laid it face down on the table. Picking up the pink envelope, she opened it and pulled out the paper inside.

She looked up at Louis, her eyes alight with pleasure once more. 'Miss Peach is having a party. She wants me to go — and you too, Daddy. Can we go? Can we?'

They looked into each other's eyes, relieved to be able to smile freely again.

'I can wear the dress with the roses on that Mummy sent me . . . ' Sofia broke off. She did not like to speak to him about Mummy, or the rose-patterned dress. There were things that made Daddy very sad. Maybe she should just leave the dress in its tissue paper until she

10

was too big to wear it.

'Of course we'll go. And the dress with the roses will be just the thing for Miss Peach's party,' Louis declared, sweeping her up and swinging her around.

He glanced down at the wedding invitation cards, thanking God for a friendly tutor and her unknowing intervention at a most timely juncture.

★   ★   ★

A few hours earlier in Fiumicino airport, whilst Louis and Sofia slept in a darkened London, all was activity and noise; a buzz of voices in an international medley of languages. It was a Monday morning and light was just seeping into the sky. The departure complex hummed and seethed like the final Saturday afternoon before Christmas in Harrods or Bloomingdales.

A small figure, jewel-bright in pink jeans and a dark blue silk shirt, shouldered her way through the throngs of towering Scandanavian businessmen stocking up on whisky and iPads in the airport shops. As the blond giants stared down, so she smiled up — and pathways melted open for her. Male attention was instantly caught; chivalry and courtesy swiftly aroused.

She was in rush, had left things a fraction too late for comfort. Her plane had been boarding for twenty minutes now and the final call had already been repeated twice, and she still needed to pay for her two lovely Italian sweaters. She joined the queue at the check-out.

A tall man in front of her was having trouble with his credit card. 'Damn thing,' he muttered crossly, patting around inside his jacket, trying to locate another card.

Over the loudspeaker a suave voice informed passengers for London Heathrow that the flight was about to leave. The tall man was still having no luck with his card. Ruefully, the girl in pink jeans abandoned her purchases on the check-out belt and made a dash for the departure gates.

A steward and stewardess watched

her with grave eyes as she clattered on her high heels down the long flight of steps. Beyond them in the darkness the plane crouched, growling urgently, engines impatient.

Running up the steps, her heart began to pump. Anticipation of flying always did that to her, for all that she was a seasoned traveller. 'Sorry, I'm late!' she told the steward standing at the door of the aircraft. He simply smiled — reassuring and noncommittal, every inch the professional.

She was pleased to have a row near the front of the plane, and the bonus of the window seat. She settled down, smoothing the creases from her jeans and noting that the seat beside her was empty. Good — she would be able to spread out herself a little; relax and sleep at ease. She clicked her seat belt shut, serene now, waiting for the doors to close and the slow trundle down to the take-off strip.

A figure erupted into the aircraft, hurling himself along the aisle, then swooping down beside her as though drawn by a magnet. She flinched.

'Here! The results of your retail therapy!' He was grinning broadly, flourishing the shiny designer bags in front of her nose.

She registered the man who had been ahead of her at the check-out. The air around him hummed and bristled as he pulled off his sweater and stuffed it in the overhead locker. He was all energy and vigour, making his presence well and truly felt.

She smiled to herself, registering the sort of man who harboured no doubts about his effortless ability to draw women into his circle of charm. And not Swedish or Danish: this man was as English as cloudy springs and rolling green meadows.

She got out her wallet and extracted a small wad of notes. 'Thank you,' she told him, proffering them.

'No, no!' he protested, gallant and expansive, waving the notes away.

'Oh, yes,' she said softly, dropping

them into his lap, then turning her shoulder to him and staring determinedly out of the window. No way would she permit herself to be patronised, however attractive the patron. Through the reflection in the thick shiny plastic she could see him flinging himself back in his seat, a lazy smile of irony curving his full mouth.

The aircraft meekly rolled to the main runway, paused, aiming its nose dead centre between the dainty rows of lights, then, with a huge roar, hurled itself forwards and up.

She felt her back pressed against the seat. And at the same time she felt the warm, dry fingers of her fellow passenger press lightly against her own, deliberately relaxed, as they lay side-by-side on the arm rest.

'Best bit of the flight,' she heard him murmur. 'Most dangerous, highest risk factor.'

She smiled, refusing to be drawn into a dialogue. Leaning her head back against her seat, she closed her eyes.

The steward came along with coffee and sandwiches. There was a choice of alcoholic drinks. Her travel companion tapped her lightly on the knuckles. 'Drink?'

She shook her head and kept her eyes tightly shut.

It had previously been in her mind to read for a while on the first stages of the flight, maybe glance over her outline for next week's work. Now with the possible threat of having to chat — and threat it was, despite the obvious appeal of her neighbour — she found herself determined to get some sleep.

She breathed deeply, recalling exercises from yoga classes some years before. She filled her lungs. Expanding, holding — and then letting go. Slowly, slowly . . .

She was walking along a broad road, but there was nothing to see — just darkness. And she was quite alone.

Flames began to lick at the road ahead, yellow and red and orange.

She put her hand to her eyes. Her hair felt hot, her eyelashes were scorched like a burned-out match. Thick billows of smoke rolled towards her and her stomach clenched with fear. Through the boiling mass of flame she made out the shape of a plane's tubular aluminium body lying on the road ahead.

With its silver belly exposed and charred, it had the appearance of a shot bird. One of the wings was tilting up to the sky. A trail of oil slithered over the wing's top surface, slimy and evil. All around the grounded plane, the air seemed to be full of moans, one long sigh of pain.

A man stumbled from the smoke. He was black from the oil and soot. Black hair, black eyebrows. Eyes like the night sky, luminous and deep beyond all imagining. But his skin was pale and milky, with a moon-like sheen.

'Oil!' he shouted. 'Oil burning! Run! Get away!'

She wanted to run away but her legs were as if sunk in buckets of sand. And at the same time she was drawn towards the man calling out warnings. He was safety, he was her only salvation. But she was stuck. The oil had slithered off the wing. Curving around the man, it began to move towards her, a snake of creeping fire.

The man was mouthing desperately, frantic to save her: Diana, Diana! But his voice simply floated away to be swallowed up in the smoke.

She was weeping now. The snake of fire was nearly on her, its tongue flicking with incandescent viciousness. As she looked with final appeal to the unknown man, she saw that he was holding out his arms . . .

Faces were leaning over her. Male faces. Terrifying strangers.

'You were kicking me nearly to death,' a dry voice informed her, springing her back into consciousness.

She stared around her, registering a plane that was airborne, thrusting calmly through peaceful, flame-free skies. Her heartbeats slowed from their violent sprinting jerks.

'And you were moaning as if a bunch of devils were after you,' her blond travel companion added. 'Get her a brandy, will you?' he asked the concerned steward. 'And one for me, too.'

'That must have been one scary dream,' he suggested. 'Fear of flying, perhaps?'

She shook her head. 'No, not at all.'

The blond man laughed. 'Well, it seems like you can have pretty spectacular dreams twenty-five thousand feet up.' He was trying to be kind. But the grasping tentacles of the cruel dream were still clinging to her.

The brandy was liquid fire in her stomach, but her body and limbs were icy cold. Squirming in her seat, she tried to get a view of the aircraft's wing. She could see nothing but the grey outline silvered by moonlight. Struck with new panic, she commanded her eyes to pierce the darkness, to see things that it was impossible to see.

In the end she had to give up. There was no way of telling if the doom-laden trail of oil was snaking its malevolent, hidden trail through the darkness. She shivered in fear. The brandy trembled in her glass.

'Hey, there! Are you okay?' The blond man turned to her. Suddenly his arms were around her, his hands holding hers, grasping tightly and steadying the violent shaking she was powerless to control. He was murmuring all manner of silly nonsense, calming her as though she were a trembling kitten.

She was grateful for his attempts to soothe her, but her body was metallic and rigid in his grasp. She felt herself shot through with dreadful warnings.

Take care, Diana! Something dreadful is coming!

2

Louis glanced around Miss Peach's sitting room, noting the creamy walls hung with landscape paintings and antique gilded mirrors. Canary-yellow curtains cascaded from ebony poles, cushions of finch green frolicked over sofas which had fat little rolls of cream velvet for arms, and crimson tassels. Pink lilies nodded their heads in large cylindrical vases, wafting pungent sweetness into the air.

Well, well, he thought, having envisaged a prim little gathering of earnest educationalists crowded into a small, neat front room drinking uninspiring white wine and nibbling crisps. Instead he was in the midst of a swirling throng, sipping champagne and biting into fragile canapés topped with caviar and tiger prawns.

'Come on, Daddy!' Sofia urged.

Maybe I should have worn a tie, Louis thought, recalling the stiff pre-lunch cocktail parties in 1980s Paris, when his mother had required him to be an immaculate accessory to her flawless chic. He put a hand up to smooth his thick black hair.

'Where's Miss Peach?' Sofia exclaimed impatiently, standing on tip-toe and peering around. 'I can't see her anywhere!'

'She'll appear soon enough,' Louis reassured her, accepting a glass of champagne from a waiter in a striped waistcoat. The first sip was cool in his mouth, with an acid sting in the tail.

Glancing down at Sofia, he laid a hand briefly on her warm glossy head, after which he helped himself to a canapé of inky squid, nestling in a lake of avocado mousse.

'Snacks for sparrows!' a voice chimed in his ear.

Louis turned. The speaker confronting him had startling blue eyes gleaming from a shaggy mane of yellow-blond hair. There was a lazy grin on the classically regular features, and yet the expression in the eyes was unmistakably challenging.

Louis found himself straightening his spine, on full alert.

'Nothing like as mundane as sparrows,' Louis commented, glancing around at the fashionably dressed party-goers. 'Peacocks, perhaps?'

The blond man threw back his head and laughed. 'Fair point.' He flung out an arm, almost toppling an approaching waiter. With a single scoop of a large hand he transferred the remaining contents of the tray onto his plate. 'Need to stock up, it could be a while before the next waiter's along,' he commented. 'They're like London buses, waiters; they hunt in packs.'

Louis gave a faint smile for the sake of politeness. He felt his lips tighten and disliked himself for his inability to relax and simply go along with whatever flow was in progress.

'Have you known Diana long?' the blond man asked.

'Who's Diana?' asked Louis.

The blue gaze sharpened for a moment. 'Our hostess.'

'Ah! Miss Peach.'

'The very same.' The man's voice slowed to a laconic drawl and Louis fancied his glittering eyes were saying, *Keep off.*

'Miss Peach!' Sofia cried suddenly, giving a little jump in the air. 'Miss Peach — I'm here.' She launched herself forward; a small missile wearing a flowered dress.

Miss Peach bent down and kissed the top of Sofia's head. Her slender arms darted around the child and hugged her. 'Sofia. My sweet little love,' she said.

The hairs at the nape of Louis' neck prickled like those of a threatened dog. Who was this young woman to call Sofia her sweet little love? That was such an affectation — gushing and false. In fact, it recalled the pet names Poppy had often called their daughter — and look where that had led. Sofia rarely saw her mother from one autumn to the next spring.

His observant gaze moved over Miss Peach, coolly appraising. As a professional photographer Louis was always at work in his head, assessing a potential subject, noting features that would become luminous on film, planning a composition.

There was something vivid and intense about this gazelle-like woman. It was not a mere question of richness of colour: the chestnut hair falling over her shoulders, the porcelain-pale skin, the flash of coral nails. There was some inner energy, some taut and fizzing quality which intrigued him.

And all of this was conveyed in the woman's gestures and body posture, for he hadn't yet seen her face — that was still bent towards Sofia, who was looking back with an animation it warmed Louis's heart to see, despite his misgivings.

'Diana loves kids,' the blond man commented to Louis, chummy now and man-to-man. 'I suppose she has to, teaching the little devils for hours at a time. It would drive me mad.'

Louis could believe it. He guessed that guns, claret and Labradors would be much more in Blue Eyes' line of country.

He gave a dry smile. There was something about this man that was beginning to grate on his sensibilities.

'Put the kid down, Diana, and come give some attention to the rest of your guests! Let me do the honours.' The speaker turned to Louis, beaming and supremely confident. He raised questioning eyebrows.

'Rogier. Louis Rogier,' Louis volunteered quietly.

'Rupert Pym,' he returned crisply. 'Diana — come on! Talk to the grown-ups. Meet Louis.'

He leaned across and took Diana's arm. Reluctantly she detached herself from Sofia and looked up.

Louis stared down, registering a heart-shaped face and large almond eyes. Diana Peach was all cheekbones and delicate translucent skin. Her hair dipped and swung as she tilted her head, and her long silver earrings glinted like moving water.

He found himself on the point of reaching for his camera in an entirely automatic gesture, but he had left it at home. Sofia had been quite firm on that point. He had not even been permitted to put it in the car.

Those lips, he thought, narrowing his eyes in assessment. So curiously tender — bare of any scrap of lipstick, they were the soft, fleshy pink of nature and the lower lip was slightly puckered like that of a child. It gave her face an air of vulnerability, which was probably quite misleading, yet utterly alluring.

But it was her eyes which claimed and held him. Perfect ovals, lustrous and haunting, and of a most unusual and compelling aquamarine. Sofia's Miss Peach was, in a word, visually mesmerising.

Louis found himself vaguely uneasy. He had expected a brisk, bright young

person, competent and professional. Someone he would take to in a detached kind
of way, grateful for her efforts to bring
out his daughter's stifled linguistic potential. He had not expected someone who
would . . . *stir* him.

Diana Peach glanced straight up into
his eyes, the polite smile of a hostess on
her face.

As Louis offered his hand in greeting,
her smile suddenly stilled and fell away.
The inky pupils of her eyes enlarged.
He had the impression that troubling
thoughts were forming in her mind. He
saw that her breath was coming in tiny,
painful gasps, and for a moment he
thought she could be on the point of
passing out.

Reaching across to her, he placed his
hand on her shoulder to steady her. She
continued staring up at him, her lips
parted slightly. The expression in her
eyes baffled him, awakening prickles of
unease.

He saw that Sofia was watching Miss
Peach anxiously, sensing something was

wrong. He recalled seeing that look in her eyes just after Poppy left. *Is it my fault?* Sofia was intensely alert to any ripple of emotions in the atmosphere.

Rupert, in contrast, seemed to have noticed nothing untoward. Grabbing fresh glasses from a passing tray, he placed one in Diana's hand, drained the other and helped himself to a second. 'This girl serves the best champagne north of the Thames,' he told Louis, grinning like a cat in a dairy.

Louis fancied that, for 'this girl', the perceptive listener should substitute 'my girl'. Rupert whoever he was was eager to stake out the ground around the intriguing Diana Peach. No subtleties here — the message was loud and clear. *Back off.*

Diana Peach had closed her eyes momentarily. She was taking deep, slow breaths. When she opened her eyes again, her mood was once again lively and warm.

'Sofia, I mustn't forget to tell your daddy how well you're getting on with your French.'

'I've noticed,' said Louis. 'Thank you.'

Diana Peach went on to elaborate, commenting on the process of the acquisition of language. She spoke of the need to build on the learning in stages, consolidating each new task and idea through a variety of interesting exercises.

Louis attended carefully. He began to appreciate that behind Diana Peach's lively, colourful exterior there seemed to be a sharp intellect. And it struck him that this young woman was not what she seemed; that she was somehow cloaking her personality behind a vividly painted screen of glamour.

Yet even as the competent professional words flowed from her, he had the notion that a part of her mind was preoccupied with something else. In addition, he was disconcertingly convinced that it had something to do with him.

Her eyes would avoid his, and then suddenly her glance would connect directly with his and with that connection would come a shock, because in her eyes was a silent scream of pain.

Louis was not a fanciful man — quite the opposite. He had always regarded himself as one of life's pragmatists, someone who got on with the here and now, tackling problems as they arose. Yet looking at the outwardly calm Diana Peach, he was sure that some turmoil was seething within her.

Sofia stood between the two of them, listening with an expression of great concentration. As Miss Peach concluded her little speech, Sofia scratched the tip of her nose and looked thoughtful, but before she could voice the question that was forming on her lips, Rupert took Diana firmly by the arm and bore her away to be swallowed up in the swirl of her guests.

Louis thought it was time to leave. 'Let's go to your favourite Italian restaurant and get a pizza inside us,' he said to Sofia.

'No. Tagliatelle,' declared Sofia. 'The green sort, with red peppers in the sauce.'

'Hot chocolate fudge cake to follow,' said Louis.

'Scrummy,' agreed Sofia.

They went down the broad steps between the stately white columns; a father and his daughter, outwardly laughing and carefree, yet in their hearts fiercely clinging to each other in their separate loneliness.

* * *

In the busy, cosy restaurant, Louis placed their order and then sat back watching Sofia drink fresh orange juice through a straw; as neat and fastidious as a cat.

Like Sofia's, his mind was still at Diana Peach's smart party. Questions revolved in his head — the issue of why a young woman, surrounded by all the trappings of seemingly considerable wealth, should spend her days tutoring the more needy members of the school population. The puzzle of why that woman seemed to enjoy the company of a macho escort who appeared somewhat challenged in the area of human sensitivity.

Yet those issues were just idle speculation. There was one of much greater significance which became increasingly disconcerting, the more he examined it. The question of why the sight of him, Louis Rogier, should arouse such naked terror in a woman who had never laid eyes on him before.

★　★　★

'Hey! Let me take you away from all this!' Lounging on one of Diana's comfortable sofas after the catering team had cleared up the plates and glasses and left, Rupert was wondering how on earth he was going to persuade her to come out on a date with him.

It was two weeks since they had shared a flight back from Rome and still she was resisting anything beyond a quick drink at the local wine bar after she finished work.

'It's Sunday,' Diana observed. 'Time

to get ready for the working week ahead.'

Rupert frowned. He was never quite sure what to make of Diana's clipped comments. Was she mocking him for his laid-back lifestyle; the way he got into work late and finished early? Or was she mocking his spoiled life as the son of a merchant banker? Or simply mocking *him*?

'Oh, come on! One quick drink at the pub down the road,' he urged her. 'Or I'll take you to Claridges if that suits you better.'

She smiled and shook her head.

Rupert fell silent. He felt like he used to as a little boy when someone managed to thwart him.

Diana gave a little sigh. She shook off her strappy platform shoes and tucked her slender legs beneath her.

Watching her, Rupert decided that Diana Peach was the most gorgeous girl he'd laid eyes on in months. There was no trace of the bimbo about her, nor was she a raving intellectual quoting

Shakespeare at him, which was what had driven him from the arms of his last girlfriend.

'Well, if you don't fancy going out, let's just stay in,' he said.

Diana was thinking how she just fancied Rupert going away and leaving her in peace. She was tired and she had a full programme of teaching the next day. She wanted to go over her preparation notes and make sure her programme was stimulating enough to capture the children's imagination.

'Well?' Rupert insisted.

'I'm whacked,' she told him gently. 'Go and find someone more frisky and obliging to play with, Rupert.'

He paused, considering his next move, and then he got up, finally realising he was not going to get his own way. Not tonight, at least. 'Tomorrow then,' he decreed. 'Supper, the theatre, drinks afterwards.'

Diana sighed.

'We are friends, aren't we?' Rupert said, winning and boyish.

She nodded.

'It must have been fate that we met in deeply romantic Rome,' he said. He moved close to her and put on his most intimate and seductive voice. 'On the plane I really got the feeling there was something going on between us.' He laid his hand on her shoulder.

Diana held herself rigid. 'I was grateful for your help and concern,' she said softly.

Rupert was baffled and intrigued. He had always prided himself on the ease with which he attracted women. But Diana Peach was showing no signs of being bowled over.

He frowned as he looked at her, a still, silent figure, her eyes staring ahead, lost in some world of her own. Suddenly he was impatient, his mind beginning to run through the list of companions he could call up on his mobile. He got up.

'I can see you're bushed,' he said. 'I'll leave you in peace. Be in touch tomorrow.'

She smiled absently.

He got up and touched the crown of her head as he walked away. 'Penny for them,' he said lightly, magnificently misjudging the mood.

Diana sat in silence. An hour passed and then another, her mind swimming with images from the past, and speculation about the future.

Since the night of the terrifying dream on the plane, she had found herself inhabiting a new internal world. Notions of death and tragedy were constantly with her. Every day she listened anxiously to the news bulletins on the radio and scanned the internet and the newspapers for a report of some shocking air disaster. She was convinced that her dream had been some kind of prediction. The image had been so powerful and vivid; it must surely have been sent as some kind of warning.

But for whom? She felt a responsibility to take action; to warn someone. She had tentatively broached the issue of premonitions in the staff room of one of the schools she visited, hoping

37

for some kind of guidance. But there had been a general consensus that 'all that kind of thing' was hysterical nonsense cooked up by charlatans or pathetic neurotics.

After a week or two, she had felt drained and weary with anxiety and indecision. She had considered cancelling her party, but then that was such a negative thing to do, and she always gave a party in the last week of February in memory of her mother's birthday. Her sweet, scatty, indulged mother who had regarded giving parties as one of life's necessities.

In fact, the party had helped at first; being with friends and circulating, laughing and playing the role of hostess had temporarily pushed away the images of tragedy and death — and then Louis Rogier had appeared and her mind had screamed back into painful alertness.

It had never occurred to her that the crystal-sharp image of the man in her dream would translate itself into reality. She had thought the figure was some kind of symbol; a healing figure sent to deal with the aftermath of tragedy. Now it seemed that perhaps Louis Rogier himself might be the one at risk. Or Sofia.

Her heart jumped and twisted. No! Not little Sofia.

3

Louis spread the prints out on the desk: lavish colour photographs of luxurious interiors of the homes of celebrities, forming a backdrop for a variety of beautiful faces who smiled with creamy assurance into Louis' camera.

Louis had that rare knack of enabling his photographic subjects to be completely themselves, to reveal their inner personality traits on film — even if they would have preferred not to. A senior editor in one of Britain's glossiest magazines had paid him a considerable sum for his previous set of shots, and for this current collection she had promised even more.

A further shoot was arranged for next week in some stately home in Kent. Louis did not yet have details of the place or its occupants. Nor did he particularly care; these glamorous assignments gave him little artistic satisfaction and he would not have chosen to do them, but for an urgent need for the kind of money Poppy had expected from the divorce settlement.

His lawyer had said he was mad to go along with her extravagant requests and had told Louis he should contest his wife's demands; after all, she was the one who had broken up the marriage and left him for another man, but Louis had not had the heart to fight her. He had never denied her anything throughout their time together and the old habits of loving and protecting her still persisted, even in the face of Poppy's rejection and what even he had eventually been forced to admit was simple greed. And now Louis was saddled with expenses which threatened to cripple him if he didn't pull out all the stops to earn every penny he could get.

Since Sofia was at school, he gave in to the guilty pleasure of lighting a cigarette and looked down at the brash, gleaming photographs. Rows of perfect snow-white celebrity teeth grinned back at him. With a little growl of frustration, he swept them to one side, then reached into his folder for another set of pictures.

These prints were in monochrome; twenty portraits he had taken during a recent visit to a local nursing home for the elderly.

A gallery of faces, grooved and gnarled like the bark of ancient trees, stared into the lens of his camera. They had all been quite happy to be photographed, but the emotions he had caught were raw and bleak. There were few smiles; rather, intimations of stoic resignation. And there was anger too, and bitter-ness, and naked fear.

Yet despite all the pain, there was something in these pictures which excited him. He knew he had captured some universal quality of human experience in these portraits; feelings that would surely touch a nerve in every observer who looked at them. The human worth of these images far outstripped that of his roll-call of glitzy celebrities, yet the money he would get for them would in no way reflect that. The bristly, wrinkled faces of nobodies waiting to die would fetch comparative peanuts.

His gaze shifted to the tall window in his room as he registered the flash of a bright yellow car. It slowed down, a slab of metallic custard seemingly intent on parking outside his house. He heard the purr of a precision engine and a little growl before it was turned off.

The woman who got out was as glowing and colourful as her car. A scarlet wrap was thrown around her shoulders and long silver earrings flashed beneath her thick curtain of chestnut hair. Louis' eyes moved over her, drawn and intrigued. Then suddenly, recognition dawned. Diana Peach, Sofia's favourite teacher.

He ran a hand through his hair and frowned. What could she want? He went to the door, opening it as she walked up the path. She looked at him and he saw her hesitation, how she drew back a little, her eyes wide like a startled deer.

He beckoned her forward. 'Please — come in.'

She walked ahead of him into his study. He smelled her sharp, peppery perfume, the warmth of her skin. The air in the room seemed to brighten, to move and flicker around her.

'Is there some problem with Sofia?' he asked in level, neutral tones.

Diana Peach looked straight up into his eyes. 'She's a little quiet at the moment,' she commented after a pause.

Louis had the impression she was struggling with some difficulty in speaking to him frankly. Uncertainty flowed from her.

'But she is still making good progress?' he asked.

She frowned, seeming distracted. 'I'm sorry?' She stared at him, clearly having lost the thread of what she was going to say.

'Sofia,' he prompted, 'are you pleased with her work?'

'Yes . . . Oh yes, she has a natural

ability with languages.'

'I agree. She just had a bad start, that's all.' He smiled, wondering what was behind this visit. 'Anyway, I'm pleased to hear she's doing well. I thought there must be some problem.'

'Well, she has been — rather quiet recently,' Diana Peach repeated slowly.

'Yes. Can't you guess why?' He gave a small grin, but she did not respond at all. Louis was suddenly exasperated. He wanted to grasp Diana Peach's shoulders and rattle her back into full alertness of the present.

'Sofia has got the idea that if she speaks up too readily she'll no longer have any need to come to your group,' he explained. 'If she's too clever a pupil, you'll throw her out — that's how she sees it. And she'd hate that — because you're one of her favourite people.' He raised an eyebrow.

Diana took a few moments to digest this information. 'Oh, of course! Why didn't I think of that?'

In the face of her continuing unease,

Louis was suddenly wary himself. 'Are you concerned about her welfare? Here at home? I know that fathers bringing up their daughters on their own are natural targets of suspicion.'

Her eyes widened in dismay. 'No! I never thought of anything like that. I've always had the feeling you and Sofia are very close and in harmony. You seem to have a really good life together.'

'Quite.' He paused. 'Well, Miss Peach,' he said crisply. 'If you haven't come to talk to me about Sofia's progress or concerns about her welfare, then what you have come for?'

She clasped her hands tightly, seemingly unable to speak. Moving away from him as though she were sleepwalking, she went to stand beside the table and looked down at the photographs. She stood for a long time, perfectly still. 'These are beautiful. Is your work — you're a photographer?' she said.

He nodded.

'Sofia told me you took pictures, but I didn't realise you were a professional.'

She picked up a print showing a smiling blonde young woman; a top fashion model, wearing simple denim jeans and a plain white T-shirt, accentuating her golden radiance.

'She photographs marvellously,' Diana commented. 'Although she's even more stunning in the flesh.'

'She's a friend of yours?' Louis enquired.

'I see her at parties sometimes.'

'You move in exalted circles,' Louis commented, not bothering to conceal a touch of sarcasm in his tone. Looking at her standing there, so immaculate and expensively turned out, he felt a small stab of rage within him towards all the spoiled women he had known.

He thought of his mother; always demanding, wanting, getting. His mother must always have new clothes, new jewels, fresh amusements, everyone's attention. And then there was Poppy. It seemed he had never succeeded in giving her enough, even though he had offered his heart and soul.

Diana looked up at him, connecting

instantly with his dark inner mood. Her eyes looked wounded and he was thrown off balance as if he had lashed out at her with no reason or warning.

'I have a lot of social connections from the past,' she said hesitantly. 'My mother knew a lot of people. That's no sin.'

'I'm sorry,' he said quietly.

She smiled, a long slow smile, her lips indescribably sweet, so that he felt a total rat for his mean remark. 'Do you believe in the power of dreams?' she asked suddenly.

He shrugged. 'I've never given it a thought.' He looked at her curiously. She was deathly pale, her eyes huge shiny pools in her delicate face.

'Premonitions,' she added, her voice unsteady.

At that he gave a dismissive laugh, making his opinion painfully clear.

'No, please! Please listen to me.'

He heard a note of naked need in her voice and gave her his full attention. 'Go on,' he encouraged softly.

'There was a terrible accident. A fire . . . ' She looked at him, terrified and pleading. 'An air crash . . . you were there . . . '

'What?'

'In my dream — you were there.' Her eyes were filled with suppressed feeling.

His emotions were suddenly roused — sympathy, curiosity, irritation, and most disturbingly, attraction. 'There are plenty of men around who might fit my description,' he said, keeping his voice calm and even.

'No, it was you. I saw you quite clearly in my dream, weeks before I met you,' she insisted.

'That's nonsense!' He sighed, exasperated.

'No, it's true.' She stared up into his face. 'That's why I was so shocked when I saw you at the party.'

He was on the point of making some disdainful quip, but glancing at Diana's stricken expression, he stopped himself. 'You've known Sofia for some time. We're father and daughter. Maybe you'd seen similarities without realising.'

'No. Besides, you're not much alike in looks.'

Louis gave a sigh of impatience. 'This all seems bizarre.'

Her head drooped. 'I'm sorry. There was no other way to tell you about this.'

'Probably not. But why bother to tell me at all?'

She gazed at him, frowning. He noticed that her skin had the delicacy of bone china and was amazed to find himself longing to reach out and touch it.

'To warn you,' she said, biting her lip.

'Warn me? Look, Miss Peach, I think this conversation is getting out of hand — '

'Are you planning to fly in the near future?' she cut in.

'Sofia and I are going to New York for a wedding. I don't lead the kind of life that includes the luxury of sailing across the Atlantic for a brief visit,' he said sarcastically, instantly regretting it as he watched her face.

'You mustn't,' she said urgently. 'You mustn't fly.'

'To the States? Anywhere? Ever again?' he asked, his flippancy laced with mounting incredulity and anger.

She sighed, then turned away from him. 'I don't know. I just know you mustn't fly to this wedding.' She faced him again, determined and defiant now. 'At least don't take Sofia. You owe her that — not to put her in any kind of danger.'

Louis' dark eyes snapped with fury. 'For Heaven's sake! This has gone on long enough.'

'You must listen to me,' she insisted, her eyes pleading. 'This isn't just a silly whim.'

'It all sounds pretty crazy to me,' he said dismissively.

She shook her head sadly. 'No. I just know that my dream is a prediction. A warning of something terrible about to happen.'

He lifted the palms of his hands in a gesture of total dismissal and rejection and she gave a sigh of defeat. Her glance moved from him and rested again on the photographs.

Louis tracked her gaze. 'This is reality,' he said brutally, sweeping his arm over the bleak, monochrome photographs. 'These people have no room for dreams and fantasy. They're too busy confronting reality, trying to survive.'

She stiffened, then suddenly she began to shake violently, wrapping her arms around herself. He heard her whisper through white lips, 'Help me — please help me!'

Louis stepped forward, appalled to witness such naked distress. It was as though he could smell this woman's pain and fear. Something cool and unyielding in him, a barrier which had lain there like a hard slab ever since Poppy left, suddenly slid softly away. He reached out to Diana Peach and put his arms around her, reassuring and comforting.

4

Poppy Rogier, soon to be Poppy King, surveyed the results of several days spent arranging and hanging canvases around the stark white walls of her penthouse gallery. This was her first public exhibition, and she was determined that it would be a success. It was going to demonstrate to the most prestigious of New York's art critics that the King Gallery was one to sit up and take notice of.

One of Poppy's best-selling lines was a series of paintings of female nudes, created by an unknown artist who lived in one of the more run-down areas of London. The big canvases were thickly textured and wonderfully rich in colour, almost luminous against the plain gallery walls. The flesh tones of the subjects, bathed in autumn-gold sunlight, breathed sensuality — speaking of warm evenings in Tuscany, of mulberry-coloured wine and nights spent in lovemaking.

It was Louis who had discovered her some years before, while visiting a back street junk shop where some of the first pictures had ended up. He had taken a sample of the young woman's work to show Poppy, who had spotted the marketing potential instantly.

'Utterly spontaneous!' she had commented. 'Totally simplistic and naive, of course.'

'They are painted from the heart,' Louis had observed drily. 'Unlike those calculated daubs by the artists you encourage.'

'They'll sell, I suppose,' Poppy had responded, ignoring the little barb. 'How many more does she have?'

'Quite a little store; she's been painting for years.'

When Poppy's contact in Paris had sold samples straight off for considerable sums, Poppy had been delighted that there was such a stash to plunder, though she never told Louis about that, knowing how he liked to champion the underdogs of this world.

Of course, this had endeared him to Poppy when they first met. He had been wonderfully bold and fearless, venturing out on shoots to collect illicit pictures of those in the Paris underworld whom the press wanted to expose. On more than one occasion, having been spotted by his target, he had arrived home bruised and bleeding, but he'd always got the pictures he wanted, lending weight to the process of justice.

Poppy knew now that she had confused determination and ambition with the desire to forge ahead and make a great deal of money. Louis had the first, but not the second.

Oh yes, he had provided her and Sofia with a very good lifestyle, but he had never been interested in serious money. In the end he had turned out rather like his father; dark and mysterious — and very French.

Her little reverie ended as her assistant, Gaby, came in with the mail. 'More wedding replies,' she announced. 'And some letters from England.'

Poppy searched through the bundle, looking for Sofia's handwriting. A spark of guilt sprang up to reproach her for choosing to leave her child in order to be with her lover. Leaving Sofia had been the hardest part of the separation. She was such a beautiful, docile child, although showing few signs of the cleverness Poppy knew she had in her.

Of course Louis was far too liberal, becoming less interested every day in the fierce competitiveness necessary for surviving in a modern world.

Recognising Sofia's writing, Poppy slit open the envelope and took out the card inside. She was pleased to see that Sofia's ability to form her letters was much improved, and her little drawings were charming. Sofia wrote to say that she and Daddy would be coming to Mummy's wedding on an aeroplane. She had news about a boy at school who shouted a lot, and a lady next door who had a dog.

Poppy scanned quickly down the lines looking for something more interesting. There was a drawing of a woman with long chestnut hair and vividly coloured clothes. *This is Miss Peach*, Sofia had written. *She is pritty and smily and I lyk her verry much.* The last two words were heavily underlined.

Poppy frowned. She felt a sudden nasty jerk of uncertainty, a feeling of anger, a sense of disbelief and — oh, horrors — jealousy! Suddenly she missed her little girl dreadfully.

'Miss Peach!' she exclaimed aloud suddenly, making Gaby turn round curiously. Poppy picked up her phone and punched in Louis' number, tapping her foot impatiently as she muttered, 'Come on — answer!'

* * *

Diana sat facing Rupert across a tiny table in a chic little restaurant in the

West End. Rupert had already polished off his Mediterranean fish soup and was now savouring his Sancerre and anticipating the roast duck, which would arrive once Diana had made her way through a modest slice of melon, filled with Cointreau-soaked raspberries.

He thought she looked enchanting and irresistible, her chestnut hair silky and bright against her china-pale skin. He just wished she would eat a little more — and rather more quickly.

In fact Diana was finding eating quite an effort. In the weeks since her dream, her appetite had gradually decreased. And since her encounter with Louis Rogier that afternoon, her interest in food seemed to have completely vanished. However she didn't want to offend Rupert, who had been extremely generous and attentive in his efforts to entertain her.

She found Rupert an amiable and amusing companion. He was low-key and relaxed and wasted no time on self-doubt or troubling himself with a consideration of the human condition and its many facets. If challenged, he would recognise that some people had all the bad luck. But for him, life was a banquet and he had every intention of enjoying it to the full.

Diana found his confidence and his carefree approach to life curiously reassuring, having been brought up by a mother who had been plagued with all kinds of doubt and worries. In addition Rupert was not prone to moods and you never had to guess what he was thinking, as he simply said it all out loud.

'Bought a new yearling this morning on behalf of one of my clients,' Rupert said, making no secret of the fact that he was much more interested in bloodstock than merchant banking. 'A black stallion, eighteen hands — a real goer.'

Diana was interested. She had a natural affection for animals, although she did not keep a pet herself at the moment as she was out so much of the time.

'I haven't ridden for ages,' she said

with a smile, recalling hectic gymkhanas and brave, wild-eyed ponies.

'Well, that's something else for me to put right in your life,' Rupert said, narrowing his eyes seductively, clearly thinking of activities rather more intriguing and intimate than horse-riding.

'I thought you were at the office this morning,' Diana said, not rising to the bait.

'Sure. I did the deal by phone. I'd already been down to the stables a couple of times with the client last weekend.' He stared hard at her. 'I told you.'

She gave a little start. 'Yes, of course. I'm sorry.' She felt her pulse quicken. She must try to concentrate on the realities of life, instead of spending the time locked in her own private world, half attending to what people said and then forgetting.

She returned to her efforts with the melon. In her head, a picture of Louis Rogier rose up, stern and priest-like as he listened to the account of her dream. And then how his disdain had softened, how his eyes had darkened and filled with compassion as he moved to enfold her in his arms, holding her close and allowing her to feel truly safe for the first time in what seemed like an age.

She shook herself back into the present, her body tingling with feeling. She took up her spoon and toyed with the little mound of raspberries.

Rupert shook his head in mock despair. 'For goodness' sake, Diana, either eat that stuff or ditch it, will you. I'm desperate for my duck!'

At the end of the evening Rupert drove Diana back to her house. He waited for her to ask him in, although he knew there was little chance of engaging in any light-hearted kissing and cuddling, the kind of thing which could lead to more interesting activities — but there was always hope.

Diana seemed to be out of bounds, untouchable. She would spend time with him, talk and listen and show promising signs of interest and affection, but still he could not bring himself to take things further. She would give him a sweet goodnight kiss and wind her arms around his neck. *That was nice,* she seemed to say, *but that is all.* If his friends knew what was going on — or rather not going on — they would be totally amazed.

Tonight, however, she did not even ask him in. He saw that she was distracted again, engrossed in her own inner world.

'Tomorrow night?' he asked.

She blinked, as though she had forgotten he was there. 'Yes,' she said vaguely. 'Give me a call.'

Rupert touched her cheek lightly, making no effort to kiss her. Getting into his car, he thought things might be moved along by his taking someone else out to dinner the following evening.

★   ★   ★

Diana ran herself a bath and as she peeled off her clothes, the dark image of Louis Rogier flashed across her inner vision as she recalled once again the feel of his arms around her.

Just the memory of his calmness, strength and integrity calmed her. She slipped into the warm, scented water and lay down, resting her head against the edge of the bath. She made herself relax and prepare for sleep.

She was now truly longing for the simple healing comfort of a good night's sleep, but at the same time, she had come to fear sleep, of being exposed to further terrifying dreams.

★   ★   ★

Louis stood at the window of the fourth-floor offices of *Now* magazine. Behind him his editor, Mary Cartland, looked through his latest collection of celebrity photographs. 'These are great,' she said warmly.

Louis leaned moodily against the thick plate glass. To the east, he could see down the river as far as the Dartford Bridge. Huge, monolithic glass buildings put up in the 1980s reared up from the banks of the river, a vast glass sea in which the refection of soft white clouds gently drifted.

'We'll run them next week,' Mary said. 'How soon can you let me have some more?'

Louis shrugged. He was tired. He had slept fitfully the night before, brooding on Diana Peach's visit and her astonishing revelation of a premonition involving himself and Sofia — all of which had been pretty unnerving. Then had come the strong feeling of connection when he'd held her in his arms; emotions he had not experienced since the early magic days with Poppy.

'Louis?' Mary prompted.

'Sorry, I was miles away.' He gave a rueful smile which made Mary's heart jerk. Not for the first time, she wondered if Louis had any idea of his effect on women. His unawareness of his dark, esoteric magnetism merely accentuated his charisma.

Mary swept her hand over the row of glossy prints. 'Your heart isn't in this work, is it?'

Louis gave a dry smile. 'You don't

turn down work that pulls in the kind of money this does.'

Mary smiled. 'We all have to compromise,' she said briskly. 'Your work is beautiful and professional — a real circulation booster. Just because things appeal to popular taste, doesn't mean one has to scorn them.'

Louis gave an internal sigh. The idea of trailing off to charm more egotistical celebrities depressed him, but Mary was absolutely right. He smiled and raised a self-deprecating eyebrow. 'I'll try to be less arrogant in future.'

'No worries,' she said. 'I'll call you later and give you the details of the shoot at Hartsford House.' She eyed him curiously. 'Louis, are you okay?'

'Yeah, fine.'

Mary was sympathetic; being a single parent was no picnic, and she should know.

'Well you just take care,' she said, ushering him through the door and congratulating herself on holding back from giving his rear an affectionate pat.

* * *

Louis walked to the nearby underground station, feeling an impulse to shake himself like a dog and somehow be free of this troubled mood and back to his rational self. He preferred to stay cool and detached both in his personal and professional life. Sofia being the one exception.

He was reminded that his daughter was still edgy and upset, worrying about her mother's forthcoming marriage and the danger of being taken out of Miss Peach's special tutor group.

Then, to make matters worse, Poppy had called him the evening before, on the rampage. Normally when she called she spent most of her time chatting with Sofia, trying to amuse and charm her child in the faintly desperate and vulnerable way parents do when they have virtually rejected their offspring.

This time Poppy had speedily concluded her conversation with Sofia; it was Louis she had wanted to speak with.

A cold rage against Poppy stirred in his heart and he realised the emotion had been building for some time. At first, he had felt sad and regretful on Sofia's account that Poppy was no longer around, but gradually the regret turned to anger and disapproval.

Then seeing the connection between Sofia and Miss Peach at the champagne party had given him a real jolt. It had occurred to him that there was a warm glow of unconditional affection between Sofia and Diana that had never been evident with Poppy. With Miss Peach, Sofia felt no need to strive to please — she simply loved to be with her.

It was over Diana Peach that he and Poppy, separated by thousands of miles of ocean and an ever-growing emotional gulf, had become embroiled in an acrimonious exchange.

'Louis!' Poppy had begun — challenging him the way his mother did when he was a small boy who had unknowingly sinned and must now be admonished.

'I'm here, Poppy. Go on.'

'Sofia has sent me an odd letter. Is she all right?'

'Sofia is fine, Poppy,' he said wearily. *As well as a kid can be when her mother's run off halfway round the world and more or less ignores her*, he thought.

'She says there's a child in her class who shouts out.'

'Yes, but I don't think it's serious.'

'She'll never learn anything if she's with disruptive children. Really, Louis, this insistence on educating her in a state school is ridiculous. I put her name down for Queen Anne's Preparatory the week she was born. It's high time she took up her place.'

'I know how you feel about this,' Louis said evenly. 'But she's very happy where she is.'

'Her spelling is a disgrace.'

'No,' Louis countered. 'Sofia's spelling is perfectly acceptable for a child of her age.'

'I don't want her to be *acceptable*,' Poppy yelled, completely losing her cool. 'I want her to be *exceptional*, the best.'

'She is,' Louis said. 'Your own child always is.'

'Oh, for Heaven's sake!' Poppy exclaimed.

'Look, Poppy, Sofia is getting along very nicely. The head teacher is very pleased with her and so is her language tutor.'

There was a short silence.

'Is that Miss Peach?' Poppy enquired, and Louis could tell she was making a huge effort to sound calm.

'Yes.' Louis held himself rigid, as though Poppy might see into his thoughts and feelings and instantly set out to trample on the tender shoot of connection which had sprung up between him and Diana.

'Louis!' There it was again, his mother's voice. Why had he never noticed it before? 'Are you and Miss Peach . . . *involved* in some way?'

Louis' breath caught in his throat as he realised that Poppy's suspicions held an element of truth. Anger took over. How dare Poppy interfere with his life? She had all but wiped him out with her infidelity and desertion. What right had she to question his new friendships?

He allowed the silence to lengthen, knowing that Poppy would be infuriated. 'I have my own friends, Poppy,' he ventured enigmatically. 'And you have Liam.'

'I have a right to know who you're going around with when my daughter is involved,' Poppy snapped menacingly.

Louis had a sudden curious sense of becoming finally severed from Poppy, as if the silken cord that had bound the two of them had drawn out thinly, frayed and suddenly given way.

'Well, you'd be delighted with Diana Peach as an escort for either myself or Sofia. She's very well educated, very intelligent, speaks several languages fluently and has the kind of friends who look as though they've popped out of London's top drawer. Exactly the kind of person you'd approve of, Poppy.'

He hadn't quite believed his ears as he heard himself making this droll speech. Poppy was certainly not impressed as she let out a choked exclamation of rage and ended the call, leaving Louis feeling not only finally cut adrift from his ex-wife, but in some way irrevocably linked with Diana Peach.

* * *

Walking down the road to his house after work next day, Louis attempted to put both Poppy and Diana out of his mind. Brooding about relationships led nowhere, as far as he was concerned — it certainly hadn't when Poppy left.

Did he really want to get 'involved' and possibly hurt all over again? No — he decided it would be best now if there was room in his life only for work and for Sofia. If he filled his diary with assignments and maintained the highest professional standards, then together with the love and care he lavished on little Sofia there would be no time left for him to brood.

On reaching home, he went to the kitchen to put some coffee on and was surprised to hear a sharp rapping on the front door.

A striking, vaguely familiar figure with a wild silver mane and long legs encased in battered vintage jeans stood on the step. Her face was shrewd and lined; he judged her to be somewhere between fifty and sixty.

'I'm Marisa Jarvis, your neighbour from across the road. I have your daughter Sofia round at my place,' she said.

Louis stared blankly at her, this stranger who had taken Sofia into her house.

'I was coming back from a walk with my dog,' she explained. 'I noticed her standing at your front door looking a bit worried.'

'Oh God!' Louis exclaimed, stricken. 'She came home early and I wasn't here for her!'

'She hasn't come to any harm,' his neighbour said soothingly. 'And no parent can be there for their child twenty-four seven.'

'But why isn't she at school?' Alarm bells began to ring in his head. 'Is she ill?' Concern for his child suddenly filled his world, making everything else seem irrelevant.

'She's perfectly fit and well,' Marisa said patiently. 'From what I can gather she's just taken a little break from school.'

He made himself calm down. 'A little break! But why would she come out of school?'

'Ah, well — that took a little time to find out,' Marisa said. 'She just wanted to sit with my little dog for a while, cuddling him. So I left her to it, until eventually she wanted to talk. She had strange little tale to tell about her teacher. Apparently Miss Peach had caused quite a stir by passing out on the floor in the middle of giving a lesson. The head teacher called an ambulance and Miss Peach was duly whisked off. Sofia was set to go to the ambulance to wave goodbye, but the head wouldn't allow it.'

Louis shook his head, and raked his hand through his hair. 'Yes, I can see that Sofia would have been pretty frustrated.'

'From how she told it, that was absolutely the case. She raged a bit and cried a bit, then seized her chance at lunchtime when the dinner ladies were at the other side of the playground and legged it. No one knew she'd gone until afternoon register. She seems a sharp little operator, your Sofia.'

Got some of her father's rebellion in her, Louis thought, recalling one or two of his own hair-raising bolts from school.

'Sofia's plan was to go to the hospital and find Miss Peach to make sure she was okay. But she soon realised that she didn't know which hospital she might have been taken to, or indeed where all the nearby hospitals are.'

'Ah, poor Sofia!'

'So she came home, hoping you'd be on hand with transport to oblige,' Marisa concluded with a wry grin.

Louis forced himself to smile back, trying to look as though he were passing off the incident as something fuelled by nothing more than childish impulsiveness. But he felt uneasy. Sofia's reaction seemed out of all proportion to the nature of the incident — yet Diana Peach might be truly ill.

'I think Sofia will probably sleep for an hour or so longer. She's used up a lot of energy worrying,' Marisa commented.

'Yes,' Louis agreed.

'And if you wanted to ... go anywhere, I'll be delighted to look after her until you come back. We get on famously, Sofia, me and my dog, Risk.' He felt her sharp glance assessing him, her eyes shrewd and speculative.

'Are you saying that Sofia would like me to go and check on Miss Peach?'

'Indeed I am. In fact if you don't go, I think you'll have trouble on your hands when she wakes up.' Her smile was faintly wicked, making Louis wonder what else Sofia had said.

'You're right,' he said briskly. 'I'll go on the bike, it's the quickest way of getting around in the rush hour.'

'No rush, Sofia will be safe with me,' Marisa said calmly.

Louis was already down the hallway, grabbing his crash helmet and reaching for his keys as if driven by some irresistible impulse to rescue Diana from whatever had befallen her.

5

Diana sat curled up in the corner of her sofa. Rain had been falling steadily for the past hour now and the afternoon light beyond the windows was yellowish and soupy. All was quiet except for the occasional swish of tyres over the wet Tarmac.

She leaned her head back and began to feel sleep creep up on her. She steeled herself to resist it and to stay fully awake. But her legs felt shaky and her mind distressingly imprecise.

At the hospital they had told her there was nothing clinically wrong. She had simply fainted from stress and exhaustion. They pointed out that teaching was a pretty demanding job, especially as she was travelling around the city to different schools and constantly faced with a variety of problems.

Recalling the way she had passed out

in front of her pupils, no doubt alarming and frightening them, made her wince with shame. But once the fuzzy red balls had started crossing her vision, she really had had no choice in the matter.

Rupert had texted her to say that he had to entertain a client that evening and that he would call her the next day. He had ended with an LOL and several kisses. Diana felt relieved, and then horribly lonely. Drained and exhausted, she felt there was no one she could turn to in order to share her ongoing, seemingly unending nightmare.

Suddenly there was a terrible banging and ringing in her ears. For a moment she couldn't think where she was, what time it was. Then the noises had stopped and there was a disturbing hush. She went to the front door, keenly aware that she was alone in the house.

She saw a shadow beyond the thick glass of the front door, its shape splintered into black needles by the sunburst rays carved into the plate. Gingerly she opened the door. A tall man stood there, dressed all in black — black leather jacket, black jeans and shiny biker boots.

'Louis!' she exclaimed, relief and joy welling up in waves.

He eased his way in, clasping her swaying figure and supporting her with his calm strength. Feeling the fear and tension in her slight frame, he was filled with compassion. Gently he guided her back to her sitting room and simply continued to hold her, stroking her face and her hair. She was like an injured animal yearning for reassurance.

'I think I'm going crazy,' she said. 'Do you think I'm crazy?'

'No,' he answered firmly. 'I think you're experiencing something I don't begin to understand. But you're not mad, simply stressed out.'

'Yes. Thank you for that, Louis, for trying to understand.'

He felt wretchedly inadequate. He doubted he would ever understand, but he did not doubt her. She intrigued and fascinated him. And he wanted her to become a part of his life. The idea astonished him — he had decided some time ago that he would forever remain dead to all those wonderful feelings.

'Have you had the dream again that you told me about?' he asked, curious even through his total scepticism about issues which defied rational explanation.

Diana was silent for a few moments. 'No. But last night I dreamed about my mother. She was killed three years ago — while driving her car. I was in my twenties then, but I was still something of an innocent, still living at home with my mother.'

Louis felt himself spellbound by her strange aquamarine eyes and her low, hypnotic voice. He had the feeling she was about to tell him a story which she had kept very private.

'Go on,' he said softly.

'My father died when I was ten. I didn't really know him, as he was always out working. He was the founder of a very successful building firm, and after his death my mother inherited a great deal of money. I knew straight away that it was my job to look after my mother. She was very needy and anxious, and still something of a child herself — she believed absolutely in the skill of fortune tellers and consulted them constantly. And besides, my father spelled it out to me the day before he died. 'You'll look after your mother, won't you, Diana? Promise me,' he'd said.'

That's a heavy burden to carry, Louis thought. He considered the situation in relation to Sofia, who was only a few years younger than Diana had been when this awesome task had been given to her. How would Sofia feel, he wondered, to be put in charge of his whole happiness?

'I saw it as a mission,' Diana went on. 'It seemed something exciting and heroic for me to do. I'd always loved being with my mother. She hated to be solemn, she liked to be entertained and have fun. And after my father died, that is what she did. She adored throwing parties, going to the theatre and the ballet. She loved travelling and buying beautiful clothes, and I was her dear little companion.'

'Didn't you miss having a life of your own?'

'Her life was my life,' Diana said simply. 'Her friends were my friends. It never occurred to me to think it might be odd, or to be unhappy.'

Louis was fascinated by the story, but could not help wondering where it might be leading.

'I had a child's idea that my mother would go on for ever,' Diana continued. 'I had no long-standing boyfriends but I never felt as though I was missing anything. I was happy to be my mother's best friend. And it wasn't until after her death that I became involved with a man.' She sighed.

'And?' he prompted gently.

'It was a painful experience, and it

didn't last long.' Her voice was uncharacteristically bitter. She leaned against him, as though suddenly exhausted, and he wondered if he should persuade her to go to bed and rest.

'You're very patient, listening to all this,' she said gratefully. 'What I've just told you links up with my latest dream. It was horrible reliving my mother's death.

'I don't remember having this dream before, although I've often imagined that moment she died, trying to persuade myself she had known nothing, felt nothing and that it had all been over in a split second. She was on her own in the car; I never saw her body, or the wreck of the car.' She stopped and drew in a long breath. 'But in the dream I lived it all. I saw the runaway tractor mow down her little car and pulverise it. I saw her poor, cut face and her mangled body.'

'Oh, Diana!'

'And I still can't get rid of the terrible pictures from the other dream I told you about.' She looked up at him with pitiful appeal. 'I feel as though my previous life has been some kind of preparation; as if I've been shaped in some way for a precise time in the future. It's like being a part of some complex destiny which is about to become reality.'

He frowned. Suddenly she had lost him — gone off on this idiosyncratic train of thinking which he was unable to comprehend or follow.

'Please, Louis. Don't be angry again. I can't help these thoughts. Dear God, I only wish I could.'

She laid her head against his chest, and her arms, which had lain still and lifeless as she spoke, now wound around his waist.

He held her very close, gently touching her face. They had met no more than three times and they knew little about each other, but already she held a place in his heart.

He bent his head and kissed her, very gently. Moments passed, then suddenly she pulled away from him.

'Louis — I'm afraid.'

'Of me?'

She shook her head. 'Of making love.'

He stroked her cheek. 'Diana, we're only just getting to know one another. We have all the time in the world.'

She looked down at her feet. 'Do you mean that?'

'Of course.' He tipped her face up. 'What's worrying you?' he asked tenderly.

'There was a man I used to see. I believed that I loved him and that he loved me. I was very naïve, Louis. It took me a while to find out I was just easy game. A lonely little rich girl who needed to have her education extended by getting laid.'

Louis stroked the damp tendrils of hair away from her face. 'So what happened?'

'I didn't get laid.' She gave a tiny smile of mischief.

'Did he frighten you?'

'Yes. I felt as if I was being attacked.' She grimaced. 'I suppose I led him on, letting him come to my room. I was such a fool, and in the end I punched him in the face and said I'd scream the place down if he didn't let go of me.' Another grimace. 'Just thinking about it makes me hot with shame.'

Louis was indignant. 'It sounds to me as if you were pretty heroic. He deserved all he got!'

'He didn't think the same. He said I was a tease.'

Louis snorted in disbelief. 'And what happened after that?'

'He went away in a big sulk — and I steered clear of men.' She took his hand and dropped a light kiss on it. 'Until you came along — and made me feel truly alive again.'

Louis, too, had the feeling of having experienced some kind of rebirth. He had rediscovered the ability to love a woman from the heart; and in doing so, had reawakened a part of himself that he had feared was dead.

★ ★ ★

Marisa watched Sofia as she slept on her sofa, with Risk the dog slumbering beneath her protective arm. *There is something about the serenity of a child's sleep that gives one hope*, thought Marisa. *Even at my age.*

Eventually Sofia shifted, Risk grunted and Marisa was instantly back in the present. As Sofia's eyes snapped open, she gazed gravely at Marisa and then smiled.

'How does the world look after a little nap?' Marisa asked.

Sofia stared around her, struggling to disentangle herself from the tendrils of sleep and start rebuilding the world of the here and now.

'Good,' she said. 'Where's Daddy?'

'He's gone to the hospital to check up on Miss Peach.'

Sofia gave a knowing little smile.

'Are you hungry?' Marisa asked her young charge.

'Yes.'

'What would you like?'

Sofia considered. 'An egg — baked in

a little dish with some cream and some butter. And tiny pieces of fried bread to eat with it. Daddy puts chives on the top.'

'Goodness me!'

'I'll show you,' Sofia said.

In Marisa's kitchen they got out eggs and cream and Marisa attempted to light her ancient gas oven, her ancient Aga being fit only for slow-cooking casseroles which could simmer for a day or so, and for Risk to cuddle up beside. She opened the oven door and was amazed to find the inside reasonably clean, even though she had not used it for ages. Whilst Sofia looked on in fascination she lit a taper and eventually persuaded the oven to produce some spluttering, chilly-looking blue flames.

'I don't cook much,' Marisa confessed. 'Let's go and look in the garden and see if we can find some chives.'

Sofia poked among the clay pots bunched together outside the French door, looking for something which could be chopped to sprinkle on to a baked egg.

Marisa looked down the garden, thinking she would soon need to haul the mower out of her garden shed and cut the lawn. In the late afternoon of an April day, the garden glowed with a vivid intensity. Buds had swelled from a delicate hazing over stark branches into fat knobs like babies' fingers. The grass, dampened by earlier rain, glinted and sparkled.

Marisa lifted her face and breathed in the sweet damp air.

'I've found some parsley,' Sofia called out.

'Well done you.' Marisa bent down, poising her scissors over some leggy, weary-looking parsley. 'So tell me about the mysterious Miss Peach,' she said, squinting and taking aim.

'My daddy is going to marry her,' Sofia said confidently. 'You should chop your parsley down when it starts getting long stalks like this. It won't hurt it and it'll grow back nice and bushy.'

'I'll try to remember,' Marisa said meekly. 'And does your daddy know about this — getting married?'

Sofia smiled with the calm conviction of childish certainty. 'Just me. I'm the only one who knows. As well as you, Marisa.' She smiled up at her new friend, with guileless affection. 'Are you married?' she asked with winning frankness.

'Not any more,' replied Marisa. 'My husband and I got divorced a few years ago.'

Sofia stared up at her. 'Were you sad?'

'Yes, I was. But I have two lovely grown-up children and they make me happy. But what about Miss Peach? What does she think about this idea of getting married?'

Marisa understood that in Sofia's eyes, Miss Peach's task was simply to fall in with her father's needs and wishes. And as long as she, Sofia, believed in that, it would happen.

Sofia simply gave a secret smile and commented that the oven would probably be hot by now and soon they had the egg-filled dishes inside.

Sofia applied herself to cutting bread into tiny squares to fry in the pan. She looked thoughtful. 'Actually I don't think Miss Peach knows about getting married — not yet.'

6

Diana was in love, filled with joy. She believed that Louis would show her a new life and with him, she would be able to do things she had not begun to imagine before she met him.

The horror of the past weeks, of being held in some kind of dark cage whilst her mind was attacked by some unseen aggressor, seemed to melt away in the heat of his love. Each time she was with him she began to understand why people, even previously sensible, steady people, did crazy, foolhardy things for love.

It was the same for Louis. When he kissed Diana and held her close, he felt a calm certainty about the future, and a deep contentment utterly novel to him. But Diana was curiously, although enchantingly, vague about the future. She seemed to want nothing but to live in the moment, savouring their new relationship. She had no wish to put a stamp on him and claim him: she was not a 'having' sort of person and that was delightful — but on the other hand, he was a man who liked to move things along.

'So what are we to do?' he demanded one evening while eating supper at her place, enjoying a chance to be alone.

Diana laid down her fork. 'Do? We simply go on as we are.'

'Oh, Diana, you're so sweet and honest,' he said, his eyes burning with feeling. 'And I love that, but isn't it time we made decisions about our future together?' he asked her. 'Sofia must be told that we're serious about each other.'

But Diana did not want to think of the future, or the past. She just wanted the here and now, with this wonderful man who had the power to fill her world. 'I have the feeling she already knows,' Diana said softly.

'Maybe — she is a very perceptive child. But I think it's only fair to let her know that we're thinking of a future together.'

'Yes.' She looked at him with that vulnerable appeal that was impossible to resist.

She was reflecting on how lovely things were at the moment, all three of them so happy. She and Louis and Sofia spent the weekends together, going for walks, shopping, playing endless games of Ludo, watching TV and cooking mouthwatering suppers. For the first time Diana felt part of a real family.

'There's nothing to be afraid of,' Louis said. 'Being honest isn't going to spoil our happiness. After all, she adores you.'

'She has Poppy's wedding to think of,' Diana ventured. 'That's quite a hurdle.'

'Okay,' he said. 'I can see there's nothing to gain in presenting Sofia with any other issues until Poppy's wedding is over and done with. But after that — we tell her about us.'

'Yes, you're right.' As she gazed into his face her eyes suddenly became thoughtful. She bit on her lip and looked away.

He wondered if she was still caught

up with that crazy dream and her disaster theory, although she had not mentioned it for some time. He stared at her curiously, unwilling to believe she might be a helpless victim of such foolish speculations which he considered pointless and potentially dangerous.

Diana reached for his hand. 'Louis, don't be angry with me.'

He saw the fear in her eyes, as though she had tuned into his thoughts and understood the flash of resentment in them. He felt like the most heartless of brutes.

Springing up, he pulled her onto her feet and folding her in his arms, his kisses banished her worries to a far shore.

★   ★   ★

As Rupert negotiated his way through London's early evening traffic, his thoughts strayed to Diana. He had allowed quite a few weeks to pass without making any attempt to contact her. This commendable restraint had been considerably assisted by the timely appearance of Lizzie Gluck, a pretty girl from Munich who was spending a riding holiday at the stables from which he occasionally purchased hunters on behalf of clients.

She and Rupert had hit it off together at once, eyeing each other over the neck of a steaming grey mare which he had just had out for a trial gallop. Within hours they had been clasped together in the hay barn kissing and cuddling, emerging covered in green wispy stalks.

In personality Lizzie was all that Diana was not: earthy, direct, and wonderfully available. After four exciting weeks, she had departed to Munich with a big, happy smile and barely a backward glance.

Left without a regular playmate, Rupert had found himself pondering on the disadvantages of the brief flings and one-night stands he had always so much enjoyed.

'Twenty-nine, old chap,' he told himself. Maybe now's the time to think of something more permanent and his thoughts instantly turned to a girl with some dignity and restraint; a girl who was hard to get. He dug out his mobile and pressed Diana's number. It went straight to voicemail. The sound of her clear, delicate voice made his heart give a little blip.

Later on as he called again from a wine bar in Islington, and still failed to get to speak to her, he left a crisp, short message, wondering what on earth she was up to.

Shamed to recall this outburst the next day, he decided the next step was simply to call at her house with an appropriately expensive floral offering and maybe a bottle of fizz. It never occurred to him that she would not be pleased to see him. Women had never said no to him — certainly not after being left to cool their heels for a few weeks.

He roared up to her house, annoyed to have to park his car way down the street from her front door; a black BMW motorbike was taking up that particular place. He peered at the bike with a critical eye. The registration indicated that it was a mid 1990s model, 1000cc, gleaming all over with soft leather and thick stainless steel. In pristine condition, it was probably something of a collector's item, thought Rupert, curious to spot the owner of this stylish piece of precision engineering.

He had once ridden a similar bike which had ended up at the bottom of a West of Scotland loch after a particularly lively Hogmanay. Rupert's father had put his foot down about bikes and Rupert had had to make do with a modest Golf GT until he came into his own money when he was twenty-one. Glancing down the road now at his new red Mercedes convertible, he felt a little stab of happiness.

Juggling an armful of roses and bottle of well-chilled bubbly, he sprang up the steps and pressed Diana's bell. Nothing happened. He rang again, hearing the responding buzz sounding deep inside the house. He knew she was at home — her quirky custard-coloured car glowed in the road next to the BMW bike.

He buzzed again, impatient now, as though she were deliberately keeping him waiting.

'Angel!' he exclaimed as she eventually opened the door, brandishing the roses in front of her startled face. She stared at him and, for a moment, he had the impression she did not instantly recognise him.

'Remember me?' he jested. She was looking at him as though he might be dangerous. 'Don't I get invited in?'

She gave him a watery smile and stood aside to let him pass through the door. 'Long time no see,' he commented. He thrust the bottle into her hands. 'Pop this in the fridge, darling girl, it's been getting hot and bothered in my sticky hand. You had me sweating there on the doorstep, I can tell you.'

'Oh, I'm sorry.' She looked genuinely concerned.

'It's okay, sweetheart. I could hardly blame you if you decided to give me the

most fearsome telling-off for not putting in an appearance for such an age.'
He allowed his thick forelock to fall over his eyes before tossing it back again.

'There's no need to apologise,' she said.

Rupert was inclined to agree there. 'Forgive and forget, eh?' He smiled and pressed a kiss on her cheek.

She smiled back, displaying no clear response to his kiss, either positive or negative. Grasping the bottle she went into the kitchen and placed it in the refrigerator. Rupert followed on, rubbing his hands and smiling to himself. And then he saw the table and experienced a bolt of shock.

In a flash he took in the crystal glasses standing together with dregs of wine shimmering in their bowls, the linen napkins screwed up and laid down on the table. A single red rose in a vase on the table. A scenario with which he was only too familiar, screaming out its message so brutally: intimate dinner for two.

Whilst Rupert stood gazing at Diana, deeply reproachful, a dark figure came down the hallway, silky and catlike. Rupert, frozen in disbelief, was forced to look on while Louis Rogier, gleaming in black leather, enfolded Diana in a brief, but intense embrace before exiting softly, his hand raised in brief acknowledgement of the untimely intruder.

7

As Poppy supervised the hanging for her next exhibition, she was drawing up a delicious menu for the supper she was giving at the weekend for her and Liam's friends, deciding on the shoes and jewellery she would wear with her wedding outfit the following weekend, and debating on the tricky pros and cons of making a forty-eight-hour flying visit to London to surprise her first husband before marrying the second.

Poppy enjoyed these athletic mental manoeuvres, which gave her a buzz and reminded her of her basic importance in the general swing of things.

'*Girl with Clouds* to go next to *Live Energy*,' she told her assistant, Gaby, who was perched on a ladder with two vivid canvases, wondering which painting was which; they both looked like the results of several spilled cans of paint over which a playful puppy had pranced. She hesitated, sneaking a look at the backs hopeful of finding some clue.

'Oh, leave it to me,' Poppy said crisply. 'Get online to JFK, will you, and get me a reservation on a flight to London for Sunday next and a flight back for Tuesday.'

Relieved, Gaby climbed carefully down the ladder with her cargo and went to sit at the computer.

Poppy was a tiny bit surprised with herself for finally making the decision to fly to London. She had aired the idea once or twice with Liam.

'It would be nice to see Louis and Sofia just on their own before we get married, don't you think? They must feel a tad lonely and cut off with the wedding coming up.'

'Sweetheart, you're absolutely right,' Liam had responded, imagining this idea of Poppy's must reflect some civilised routine divorced European couples liked to go through, the Europeans being such an old-fashioned and polite bunch.

'You don't mind, do you, darling? You've no need to feel jealous, you know.'

Liam had given a whimsical smile and made appropriate noises about being insanely jealous. In fact, as a rich and self-made man, he harboured no envious feelings whatsoever towards the aesthetic-sounding Louis Rogier with his heavy principles and lightweight bank balance.

Poor little Sofia and poor Louis, Poppy kept saying to herself. But all the time a mischievous and discordant voice kept whispering back that maybe her little ex-family were not so lonely and unhappy at all. They were going to transfer their affections to someone called Diana Peach — someone she knew nothing at all about, aside from Sofia's description and Louis' uncharacteristically warm remarks. Thoughts of a new woman carving out a maternal concern for her little Sofia kept rearing their ugly heads to attack Poppy's equilibrium, leaving her with an unpleasant sensation of being usurped.

Gaby returned from the computer. 'I've got you on an eight-thirty flight, Poppy. I couldn't get anything from JFK, so I've booked a flight from La Guardia. Sorry, it's a busy weekend.'

'Oh, really! What a pain, I hate that place and it's murder getting there. I'm sure you could have found something at JFK if you'd looked more carefully.'

Gaby flinched slightly under Poppy's challenging stare. 'I'm sorry, I did try. I got you a place on the helicopter link. It only takes a few minutes to get to Guardia on a Sunday morning.'

'Oh, all right,' Poppy grumbled. 'But you need to be more persistent, Gaby. Maybe you could call JFK direct and mention Liam's name. One needs to be firm with these officials. On second thoughts, don't bother. You probably won't get anywhere and I'm too busy to be wasting time arguing about bookings.'

Gaby slunk away, resolving to step up her quest to find another job. Sensing

Poppy's irritation and edginess, she wondered if her boss was truly happy to be marrying Liam King.

King might be dynamic and loaded, sexy too, in a balding, Jack Nicholson kind of way, but Gaby had been fascinated by the photograph of Poppy's little girl and her ex-husband which was propped up by the printer on her desk. She rated Louis Rogier, as drop-dead gorgeous with his sword-like cheekbones and dark brooding eyes, those long curved lips — so stern and yet so very tender. And the kid; she was a real sweetie, cute and smart and totally lovable.

Watching Poppy's frantic, intense expression now as she spoke rapidly into her mobile to Liam, at the same time checking and signing letters, Gaby wondered if her boss would have been happier if she had never left London. Gathering up the letters to fold and mail, it struck Gaby that perhaps Poppy Rogier nursed a hidden wish to return to her previous family and have a shot at good old-fashioned living happily ever after.

★ ★ ★

Flying over Manhattan in the all-round-vision helicopter shuttle, Poppy gazed down at the breathtaking panorama beneath; the countless high-rise blocks flashing their glass and steel heads in the sunshine, the glinting river snaking sinuously around their feet. Utterly breathtaking. As the helicopter dipped and then righted itself, so the great blocks swayed in a gentle dancing response. A fellow passenger clutched at his stomach and closed his eyes. Poppy smiled to herself and craned for a better view. She was always fearless when flying, adored the exhilaration of it, the speed, the risk.

At La Guardia this Sunday morning, everything seemed to be in chaos. The business-class lounge was temporarily closed, queues at the check-in desks were interminable, people were getting hot under the collar and the flight information was announcing a delay of two hours before the flight left.

Poppy stared around her in exasperated frustration at the great stew of people all around her, all simmering together.

Why am I doing this? Poppy wondered suddenly, and in a flash of insight she was finally able to look in her inner heart and admit the true motivation behind her actions. In setting out to England, the prime focus of her journey was not her 'little family' as she liked to think of her daughter and ex-husband, but simply to see Louis — her first lover, the first man with whom she had felt a strong connection.

He rose up in her thoughts, the young Louis, a photographer for a minor Paris newspaper, determined to make his way. Tall, lean-hipped, dark and faintly scruffy in his weathered, wrinkled black leather jacket, he had projected an air of supreme elegance and raw masculinity. He had presence and purpose and gravitas. She had found his cool demeanour both enticing and compelling. His calm, even temperament had seemed to hint at some dark turbulence beneath.

His demonic pursuit of his work had been a magnet to her too, although it had been precisely that dogged integrity and professionalism which had later frustrated and infuriated her.

Over a six-week summer vacation in Paris, Louis had enchanted her, and she had no doubts that he felt the same way about her. Her parents had been charmed with him too, but had not considered him good husband material. He had, after all, few assets to offer besides his considerable abilities and personal charm. And photography was hardly one of the solid and worthy professions like medicine or law.

Her parents' opposition had made him utterly necessary to Poppy's happiness, sweeping away any needling doubts. Braving her parents' disapproval, she had married him the following year, following which they had been supremely happy for another two or three. But inevitably the first heart-stopping magic had begun to fade and transform itself into something steadier — and those had been good times too, she reflected.

She supposed it was the birth of Sofia which had started them on the fatal downward slide. For the first time they had clashed about basic life issues. They simply did not agree on child-rearing methods, and as Sofia grew to be a toddler the gap in their philosophies had widened into a chasm.

Despite the difficulties, Louis had remained steadfast in his love and care for his wife. Even when she had become involved with Liam, he had persisted in loving her. At the time it had made her angry with him, because she hated to be confronted with even more guilt.

Standing in the queue to get her boarding pass she felt a shiver run through her body. *No,* she whispered, swept away with a sea of feelings dredged from the past, *no!* The power and magnetism that Louis used to have over her could never be revived. Surely not. Poppy's strong convictions were suddenly shaken up, little fragments of confetti in a stiff breeze.

As she took her boarding pass and moved along in the queue to board the plane, she had the sudden, amazing thought that she might want Louis back. The idea, once in her head, appalled her. Her first marriage was over. Boats had been burned.

Besides which, she loved Liam. She fitted with Liam; they went together, a pair. People changed, moved on, needed to form new relationships. *Yes, yes, yes!* she muttered fiercely. *Then to go is madness,* she informed herself. *Wilful and stupid.* Looking around her at the throng of people all bent on dashing around the world, Poppy had an urge to simply walk away and go back to the gallery. She could spend the day working, or call Liam and arrange lunch together.

She closed her eyes for a moment, detesting doubt and confusion. The queue propelled her relentlessly forward like a wave about to break on the shoreline. She took in a deep breath and forced herself to make an impartial decision based on reason, not emotion.

She was a strong woman, her own person. It was surely an affirmation of her affection for her daughter that made her want to share some precious moments with her before she committed herself to a man who was not her father.

Poppy stepped into the aircraft. 'Hi, there!' she said to the welcoming steward, her smile vibrant and secure.

8

Sofia had been told she could stay up a little later than usual when Marisa came to child-sit while Louis went to the theatre with Diana and then had supper at her house. It was the first time since Poppy had departed that he had left Sofia on her own with someone else.

Sofia had chatted happily over supper, asking Marisa questions about Risk and the best way to look after a pet dog. All the time Risk sat close beside Sofia, looking up at her lovingly, appreciating all the little tit-bits she kept slipping to him as she and Marisa got to grips with the toad-in-the-hole recipe.

'I think Risk likes me,' she told Marisa.

'He most certainly does.'

'Will he miss me when I go to Mummy's wedding?' Sofia asked thoughtfully.

'I should think he will.'

Sofia was silent, her face still. She stirred the mixture in her bowl with a thoughtful expression.

'Are you looking forward to the wedding?' Marisa asked.

Sofia nodded, but Marisa was unconvinced. She watched the little girl doggedly continuing to move her spoon in the batter, stirring all her hurt and bewilderment into a few broken eggs, determined to be stoical and brave.

What a hurdle for a child to face, Marisa thought — to fly halfway across the world to be a witness to the final demolition of one's family — and from what Marisa had gathered, she had not seen her mother for six months.

'Mummy sent me a dress to wear at the wedding,' Sofia said, still stirring the eggs which were now pale, creamy and foaming. 'It's blue, and I'm going to have some flowers to hold.'

'That sounds good,' Marisa commented.

'Daddy got me a dress, too.' Sofia gave a tiny smile. 'A yellow one with a green sash. Diana helped us choose it.'

'Why not wear the blue one to the wedding, and change into the yellow one for the party afterwards?' Marisa suggested, instantly grasping the child's dilemma and the impossibility — as Sofia clearly saw it — of not upsetting either parent.

Sofia put down the whisk and wiped her hands carefully on the towel Marisa had tied around her. 'That's what Daddy said,' she told Marisa solemnly.

'Well then, it must be the right choice,' Marisa agreed dryly.

Sofia sat down and rested her chin in her hand. She sighed.

'You'll have a really fun time,' Marisa said confidently, praying that it would be so. 'It will be like a big adventure, you and Daddy flying off together.'

Sofia thought about it. And then she smiled. 'I wish that Diana could come to New York too,' she said.

After supper was over, Sofia quietly disappeared upstairs with her new doggy friend. When Marisa went up later, she found them both curled up in bed, peacefully sleeping.

Smiling, she went downstairs, tidied up the kitchen and then found some music on the radio and settled down to relax. After a time she heard Louis' landline phone warbling. But the walk-about phone was not on its handset and she couldn't locate it. It soon stopped and she decided not to hunt further.

★　★　★

Poppy leaned back in her seat and gave a little sigh of relief and pleasure. The cabin staff were smiling and helpful, the atmosphere in the aircraft calm and purposeful. Another world entirely to the jumble of the airport.

She had a window seat and the place next to her had not been taken. Once in the air, she was able to relax further. The steward brought her chilled champagne and apologised for the delay in setting off. He was young and dark and appealing; Italian, Poppy guessed, hearing the faint elongation of certain vowel sounds. He came back later, enquiring about her comfort, letting her know that if there was anything she wanted, then she had only to ask him. Poppy sensed a frisson of attraction between them, and couldn't help being charmed.

Approaching the UK, the pilot reported poor visibility for landing at Heathrow. The aircraft had been given instructions to divert to Newcastle. They were to take an easterly route, flying over the English Channel and the North Sea. The weather was likely to be a touch squally and the passengers should be prepared for turbulence and fasten their seat belts, but naturally, there was no cause for concern.

Within seconds the steward was once again in attendance. 'Nothing to worry about,' he said.

'All this delay is so annoying,' Poppy responded wearily. She suspected her ankles were beginning to swell and longed to be on the ground again. The steward offered more champagne. But Poppy's head was beginning to ache now. She ordered tea instead and searched her bag for aspirins.

Flying up the north-east coast of England, the aircraft encountered vicious winds, and at the same time, when the steward looked out towards the tail of the aircraft, he saw black smoke curling over the wing.

Shortly afterwards, the aircraft disappeared from radar screens. Later it was officially reported as three hours overdue for landing.

That evening, wreckage was spotted off the Yorkshire coastline by the pilot of another flight. A search by helicopters and divers was instantly put into operation.

9

Sunday evenings had not been the best of times for Rupert in recent weeks. The leggy eighteen-year-old he had been casually dating was never available at that time, claiming quality time with her parents as the excuse.

Rupert was not so sure. Since discovering Diana with Louis Rogier — a veritable viper in the love nest Rupert had fancied he was building for himself — his confidence had undergone a noticeable setback. What if the leggy girlfriend had also suddenly discovered a preference for dark, stern-looking French guys?

Worse, he had found himself increasingly desperate to win Diana back, even while recognising that it was basically a no-hope project. Even more serious, he had found himself, almost as if willed by a mind other than his own, impelled to drive past her house one dateless

Sunday evening, not just once, but for a good half-hour, slowing down each time he passed her place, staring up hopefully and humiliating himself in the process.

What could he expect to gain from such adolescent behaviour? he asked himself irritably. He was hardly going to pound on her door and demand that she come to her senses and stay with him instead.

This particular Sunday evening he had been particularly bored and frustrated. He had driven into the vicinity of Diana's house against all injunctions from his better self not to, and when he saw the black BMW motorbike parked in the road like a brooding sentinel, he was not sure whether the intensity of his response was pain or some grotesquely masochistic pleasure.

Parking a little way down the road, he pushed a new CD into the sound system, reclined the back of his seat, then stretched out his legs and settled down for a long vigil.

★ ★ ★

Marisa woke suddenly, having fallen into a light doze. Outside the garden was disappearing into long shadows as the sun sank down below the horizon.

The phone warbled again and she felt a little stab of concern. She went upstairs and checked on Sofia, who was still sound asleep — the telephone rang again, several times and Marisa realised she would have to find it. A search of the ground floor eventually located the phone under a cushion on the sofa.

The call minder service offered her several messages. Someone called Liam King wanted to know if Poppy had arrived safely; she wasn't picking up her mobile, and maybe she'd call him when she finally made it. Later he was more urgent, wanting to know if Poppy's flight had been delayed, if she had been in touch at all. Still later he was wanting Poppy to call him back the absolute minute she got in. Then, later still, he wanted Louis to call him as soon as possible.

'For pity's sake, someone pick up this goddamn phone!' was his final message.

Marisa dialled the call-back facility and got the caller's number — a USA code, a New York number. She scribbled it down on the back of her hand. What was going on? Marisa wondered. Poppy Rogier on a flight from New York evidently not arrived yet.

She picked up the phone and punched out the New York number. Liam King was in a state of despairing frenzy. 'Is that Louis Rogier's place? Is Poppy around? For God's sake, has she arrived yet? Where is she?'

'I'm sorry,' Marisa said. 'I can't help you. I'm Louis' neighbour. He's out at the moment and I'm looking after Sofia.'

There was a low groan.

'Can you fill me in?' Marisa asked, somewhat at a loss.

Struggling to control his escalating panic, Liam introduced himself and gave a brief account of Poppy's travel plans.

'I've been watching the breaking news,' he said. 'A flight from La Guardia was diverted up the UK east coast, contact lost, aircraft now presumed missing . . . ' He lapsed into silence.

Marisa swallowed. 'Sorry — I haven't seen the news. I'll try and find out more for you.'

'Can you please try to find someone in your God-forsaken country who knows what's going on!' The voice throbbed with helpless despair before the connection was cut.

Marisa felt herself infected by Liam King's desperate anxiety. When the phone instantly warbled again she snatched it up.

'Look, I'm sorry, ma'am,' came Liam's deep voice. 'This mess, it's not down to you.'

Marisa marvelled at the speaker's courtesy even in the throes of escalating terror. 'Don't worry about it,' she said.

'Where is Louis, anyway?'

Marisa drew in a breath. 'Out with friends,' she managed.

'Yeah. He probably wouldn't know she planned on coming. She's like that,

Poppy — spontaneous.'

Arrogant was the word that sprang to Marisa's mind. And also, possibly, dead. 'Look, I promise to try to get the up-to-date news here,' she told Liam.

She tuned in to the BBC breaking news. It reported that an afternoon flight from La Guardia, diverted from Heathrow, had crashed in vicious squalls off the north-east coast of Yorkshire.

The plane's tail had been sighted, and also a number of bodies. The search by helicopters and divers was just beginning, though with the loss of natural light it might be called off and resumed at dawn. The seas were reported to be heavy, winds stiff and the temperature unusually low for early summer. A helpline number was given.

Staring at the flickering words on the screen, Marisa toyed with the idea of calling Liam back and then changed her mind, knowing that this was the point where she needed to hand on responsibility to those most closely involved. Helping out a neighbour was one thing; taking over the operation was quite another. With a heavy heart, she dialled the emergency contact number Louis had given her . . . Diana Peach's number.

10

Louis carried the mugs of fragrant coffee into Diana's airy front room, then paused by the impressive grand piano standing in the window.

'I've never heard you play,' he said to Diana, as she came through with a plate of delicious-looking chocolates.

'Oh, that was my mother's piano,' she said.

'But do you play?' he persisted, smiling.

'Yes — a little.'

'Will you play for me now?'

She hesitated. 'Yes, all right. What would you like to hear?'

He thumbed through the pile of music resting on a delicate walnut stand beside the piano. Beethoven, Schubert, Haydn, Brahms, Mozart.

'Who's the best composer?' he said with a grin of challenge.

'Mozart,' she said simply. 'I'll play you his *Rondo in A Minor*. Some critics say it's the best rondo ever written.'

Louis sat down, watching as her hands rested briefly on the keys before beginning. A most yearning, yet sharply defined melody crept into the room, the sound winding itself into his emotions. She played with such delicacy, such clarity. And then suddenly the mood changed and there were tumbling melodies shifting from one hand to the other, merging into one another like waves racing and falling to the shore.

Louis sat transfixed. He guessed that the technical problems of the piece must be considerable, and at the same time that she was a seriously talented player. What a remarkable person she was, so gifted and yet so modest. So female and wantable.

He got up and rested his hand lightly on her shoulder as she went on playing. 'This is wonderful,' he murmured.

The piece came to an end. Diana gave a little shake of her head and then stood up. They stared into each other's eyes for a few moments.

'I love you,' he said simply. 'I want you to be with me for always.'

'Yes, I know.' She smiled, kissing him lightly on his cheek.

'You most certainly should by now.' He vowed that once he and Sofia were back from Poppy's wedding, nothing would keep them apart. 'Shall I open some champagne to help the coffee down?' he asked.

'How do you know there is any?' she teased.

'There always is. Every time I've been to your place, there's always been champagne, chilling in the fridge at exactly the right temperature.' He turned to her and a glint of connection flashed between them.

She laughed. 'Only the best for you, my darling Louis.'

'Which must be why *you*'re here for me,' he said, kissing her lips. 'Now — you sit down, I'll get the champagne.'

Diana heard him in the kitchen, the

sound of the fridge door, the chink of glasses, the low 'thwup' of the cork being eased from the neck of the bottle.

He came back, bringing long, cooled glasses. They toasted each other. They toasted Poppy and Liam. They toasted Sofia and their future life together.

'When we're married, where shall we live?' he asked. 'A new place, do you think? A new start for both of us?'

'Oh, yes! It would be so good to look for a place for the three of us.' Her face glowed. 'Making a new home.'

Enlivened by the idea, they let their imaginations run riot. They would rent a little flat in town for Louis' business needs, and then buy a house in the country where Sofia could have a garden to play in. She could have a dog — maybe even a pony. Or they could settle in France, an old house in Provence close to where Louis' father lived.

'I can't wait to introduce you to my father,' Louis added. 'You two will get on really well.'

Diana laid her cheek on his shoulder.

When the phone rang she made a smiling, rueful grimace as she reached for it. Her face registered faint puzzlement, followed by brief anxiety, then smiling relief.

She held out the handset to Louis. 'For you — it's your neighbour. Don't be alarmed, Sofia is perfectly well.'

Louis spoke into the phone. 'Marisa — how are things going?'

Diana watched him with love and close attention. Gradually the smile died from her eyes. She sensed some huge change taking place in him, some massive shifts of judgements and alliances. With the powerful instinct which enabled her to tune in to the most intimate and personal emotions, she knew instantly that some terrible and fundamental event had taken place. A chill ran through her.

He said little — the occasional low growl, a 'yes', and 'I see'.

Diana stared at him, a sickening terror threading itself through her insides. She heard him say 'goodbye', his voice sounding muffled and unreal.

He turned to her, handing over the handset. Then he went into the hall and got his coat.

'Louis?' Diana's voice was just a tiny croak.

He ignored her. As his lean body disappeared into the leather coat she fancied he was withdrawing from her; body and soul.

She got up and stood beside him. 'Tell me,' she whispered. 'Please, Louis.' She reached out to him, but dared not touch.

He turned to her — not to comfort, but to confront. She shrank back, seeing the terrible pain in his face.

'Poppy is dead,' he said. 'Poppy, my wife.' He spat the words out as though they were an accusation and his eyes blazed like firearms.

Diana staggered backwards, landing awkwardly on the sofa. Her body was shaking and her heart thudding. So this was it: the horrifying reality of the grim pictures which had invaded her mind. She felt drained and empty, and in some way guilty and implicated.

'A plane? Was she on a plane?' Diana whispered, pleading with him to communicate with her.

Louis stared at her as though she were a stranger. He began to speak to her in rapid French. He gave her the necessary information with frightening impartiality and lack of emotion.

'Oh no — oh, God, no!' She wanted to throw herself at his feet and beg his forgiveness. She felt she had committed some sin and she wanted to be reassured, told that it was not so, and forgiven.

Her mind darted about, frantic and hopeless. She longed to be close to him again so that she could comfort him in his loss. But when she saw the firm set of his jaw, the hardness in his eyes, she knew that in his heart he had already moved miles away from her. Trembling, she held herself back from him with iron control.

'You,' he said eventually, calm and cool so that her blood chilled in her veins. 'You have done this.'

'No!' She crumpled under the naked brutality of his accusation. How could she bear such heavy blame?

'You believe in the power of the mind,' he observed coldly. 'How many times have you told me?'

'That doesn't make me guilty of what has happened,' she protested. But it was no more than an automatic response to defend herself. When she heard him voice her own doubts and command her to take the blame and carry guilt, she believed him. She loved him so much that whatever he said to her must be the truth.

Louis gazed down at her, hard and unrelenting. She felt them being pulled apart from each other even as they spoke. She was going to lose him.

'I have to go now,' he said, speaking in English again, as though all the important things had been said, as though everything vital was now over and done with.

She wanted to go with him, to be

there for him and Sofia. But she saw in his eyes that she was the last person he wanted to share in this tragedy.

'There are things I have to attend to,' he said formally.

'Yes . . . of course.' She watched him turn away, desolation washing over her, a cold swamping wave. As silent as a stone, he went down the hallway. He took up his crash helmet and keys from the table.

'When will I see you?' she dared to ask.

He turned, amazement on his face. He paused for a second, but made no response. Softly he moved to the door, opened it and slipped through.

Diana stood transfixed. A great black void opened within her; an unfurled black wing of grief. She sensed the breaking of bonds. She sensed endings and emptiness. Already she ached for him.

It was impossible to think. All she could do was feel. She knew that through some brutal, primitive survival system she would manage to live through the next few seconds and minutes without

Louis. And after that, she might be able to think of living through endless hours and days. Without Louis.

Slowly she sank to her knees on the silky Turkish rug covering the cold marble floor. She bowed her head.

★　★　★

Rupert returned to full consciousness with a little jerk. He had been lightly dozing; the radio had cut in after the CD finished and now it sang softly, some gently soothing night music. A serenade for sweet seduction.

He saw Diana's front door open, a narrow strip of light broaden into a wedge through which Louis Rogier stepped. Tall and ramrod-like in his leathers and helmet, he was something of a sinister figure.

Rupert snapped into acute alertness. He watched with intense concentration as Rogier ran purposefully down the steps, hauled the cover from the bike, then threw his leg over the saddle. The bike's engine activated instantly and roared away down the road in a literal cloud of smoke.

Rupert tapped his fingers on the steering wheel, pondering. What was going on? He had only managed a fleeting glimpse of Rogier's face. But he fancied there had been an expression there that suggested something was badly wrong. And there had been no looking back, no final wave of farewell.

Could this have been an abrupt exit fuelled with anger? Could he have been witnessing a flight from a lovers' quarrel? Rupert recalled a few of those, good heavens, yes! Excited speculation fizzed through his nerves. He slid out of the car, zapped the central locking and watched the car wink its lights in response.

Standing on the broad step outside Diana's door, he considered his plan of action. He raised his hand to bang on the door and lowered it again. This was no time for bullishness. Delicacy was the keynote. Softly, softly — like stalking a deer.

Placing his nose close to the glass, he peered into the hallway. The overhead chandelier was switched on, illuminating the place like a stage-set.

And centre-stage — oh, dear God — there was his fey-like little Diana; kneeling on the carpet, hands covering her face, her body shaking. Oh, the poor wretched darling! Hearing her hollow wrenching sobs, his heart somersaulted.

He tapped with his fingernails on the glass, then he pressed the bell very lightly, but she gave no sign of noticing. He supposed he could put his fist through the glass. He'd have to wrap a protective cloth around his hand first. These were not the circumstances in which one wanted to be troubled with slitting one's arteries and bleeding to death.

Knocking again with just a little more force, he discovered that the door was not fully closed. It swung back at his touch and he was able simply to walk in.

Her grief filled the hallway, echoing

in every corner, floating away into the rooms beyond and up the staircase. Terrible moans of primitive pain. He bent and touched her shoulder.

Her body stilled and her chest heaved as she took huge recuperative breaths. She turned slowly and looked up at him, for a moment seeming uncomprehending. A light of hope flickered and was snuffed. She let out a long, shaking breath. 'Rupert!' she murmured.

He pulled her to her feet, revelling in his own gentleness and the delight of holding her again.

'Oh, angel,' he murmured, stroking her hair, running his hands up and down her spine. Her body was so slender and frail. Her vulnerability stabbed at him and he made a sudden vow never to hurt her.

She crumpled against him, and the trembling through her body touched and aroused him. He was acutely aware of the spicy fragrance she always wore; it inserted itself into his senses, exotic and teasing. And beneath it were sensual notes of warm human femaleness.

Strong animal desire surged up, but he knew that he must control it. For there was something other than desire at issue regarding Diana tonight. As he held her close to him, the words 'to have and to hold' ran repeatedly through his head.

11

Louis felt the wind against his face. A raw, unforgiving wind springing out of the darkness. Behind his eyes there was a sharp and vivid picture of Poppy when he had first met her; a heady brew of mischief, wilful femininity, just a touch of the tigress. She had seemed to him a little wild when he first knew her. He had told himself that if he ever linked up with her, he would never try to tame that independent spirit.

As tears of grief and shock ran down his face in diagonal streams, he allowed himself to believe that he had been true to his silent pledge. He winced to recall the unkind thoughts which had crept into his mind about Poppy in recent weeks. He would not think of them, but cruelly the words rose up to reproach him; words like wilful, selfish, grasping. Those were the words he had used as captions to the pictures of Poppy in his head.

Ever since Diana . . .

He swerved suddenly to avoid a large plywood box lodged against the kerb. He had only just noticed it in time. *Fool,* he told himself. He could have been thrown off, injured, killed. Swearing softly, he forced himself to think of nothing except getting back in one piece to Sofia.

Marisa was standing in the open doorway, her hair like a halo under the light. 'Sofia's fast asleep. She knows nothing.'

'Then I'll leave her be.' He took off his helmet and tore open the snap fastenings on his jacket. 'Is there any more news?'

'I'm afraid it's not looking at all good. There's a number for relatives to ring.' She handed him the pad on which she'd jotted down the digits and went through to her sitting room, leaving him to himself.

She heard his voice, a low flat

murmur. When it was over, he came to sit opposite her. He put his head in his hands. Marisa sat and watched him. There was no need for him to say anything. The message in the tenseness of his body and the bleakness in his features made everything quite clear.

'They've found her body. She was wearing a locket I gave her when we first got together. It has to be Poppy . . . ' Marisa waited for him to go on. 'They need positive identification. I have to go as soon as possible tomorrow.'

'Yes.' She got up and poured him a whisky, handed it to him neat. 'Louis, you must contact Liam.'

'What?' He looked up. 'Liam. Oh. no.' He heaved himself upright, moving wearily like a much older man. At the door he turned. 'Why did she have to do this, make a flying visit to London? What on earth made her do this crazy thing?'

He was gone for ages this time. When he came back he threw himself down once more and closed his eyes. Marisa sat and watched him. There had been a number of scenes like this in her past, scenes of unspeakable anguish — a parent dying, a husband betrayed. She felt a calm stillness inside her, knowing that it was possible to survive pain and, in time, rejoin the mainstream of life.

They sat in silence for a while.

'When someone dies,' Louis said, 'you think about that person all the time. You're all choked up with regrets. You start punishing yourself because of all the mistakes you made and all the things you should have done that you didn't.'

'Yes,' Marisa agreed. 'That's what you do if you have any humanity at all.'

He closed his eyes in despairing concentration.

Marisa, watching him, had the irreverent thought that if she had been younger and he had been hers, she would have walked through fire for him. He was so finely drawn and sensitive.

'There's something else,' he went on. 'Punishing others as well as yourself.'

'Oh, yes,' Marisa agreed. 'We all of us do that, don't we? In my experience, anyway.'

He made no further comment, relapsing into silent contemplation.

'I'll give Sofia her breakfast tomorrow and take her to school,' Marisa said, mindful of practicalities. 'Will you speak to her first?'

'Yes. Oh, dear God!'

'She still has you,' Marisa pointed out. 'The parent who has been looking after her for the last two years.'

'She's only six,' he reflected. 'Children shouldn't have to lose either parent when they're so young.'

'No, but maybe for Sofia, Poppy was lost when she left you both.' She wondered how she dare say that to him at this time. She supposed she thought it was true, and it might help him.

'Do you think she'll be fit to go to school?' Louis asked.

'Children often find the daily routine reassuring at such times,' Marisa offered.

Marisa was reminded that one thing

Sofia really looked forward to was her Monday morning session in Diana Peach's language groups. She would surely be upset to miss that. Observing Louis' dark expression, she guessed that Louis was thinking along the same lines. She also understood instinctively that the subject of Diana Peach was now forbidden territory.

Louis meanwhile was doggedly battling to stop the image of Diana intruding on that of the dead Poppy and the only way of coping was to push that beloved image away and try to hate it.

★   ★   ★

Sofia sat at Marisa's table eating tiny bits of croissant. Risk sat under the table by her feet, discreetly devouring whatever was dropped his way.

Louis had wakened her very gently that morning and told her that Mummy had been in a plane crash, that Mummy had died.

Sofia had felt her father's sadness

stealing through the room like an autumn mist. She had put her arms around him and tried to make him happier. Then he had set off to the station, because he had to go on a journey to somewhere far away, but he would be back that evening.

'Will Mummy never come to see us again?' Sofia asked Marisa. 'I can see her in my head.' She screwed her eyes up tightly. 'A bit.'

Sofia pulled another doughy lump from her croissant and Risk's nose quivered. She said, 'If I collect some of those pink petals that blow off the trees in the park and wrap them in a clean hanky with the watch Mummy sent me for Christmas and put them on that big stone in the garden and count to a hundred, would she come back then?'

'No,' Marisa told her gently. 'Can you really count up to a hundred?'

'Yes — and in French, too.'

'Good for you.'

'Do you want to go to school this morning?' Marisa asked.

Sofia looked puzzled. 'I always go to school.'

'I know, but your daddy said if you would rather stay here, then that's all right.'

'It's Monday,' explained Sofia. 'Miss Peach always comes on a Monday.'

'Yes,' Marisa agreed.

'Can I tell Miss Peach about Mummy?'

Marisa looked at the solemn child and felt tears spring behind her eyelids. 'Of course you can,' she said, privately wondering if Diana would make it in to school this morning, given the circumstances. Not to mention the scene which must have taken place last night between her and Louis.

On the way to school Marisa kept a steadying hand and a close eye on her small friend. Sofia seemed to be bearing up pretty well, but then children's reactions to death were not like those of adults, she mused. Children of six still believed in magic, in some fantasy-based possibility of reincarnation.

But Marisa had a feeling that, after

Sofia had enquired about magical methods of bringing her mummy back, her reactions to being told of the impossibility of success had been tinged with a certain relief.

Oh, poor Poppy, thought Marisa. *You left to make a new life and lost your child in doing so.*

At the school gates Sofia lifted her face up for a kiss, then she kissed Marisa back.

'I'll be here to collect you this afternoon,' said Marisa.

Sofia moved forward to join the throng. Suddenly she ran back and wrapped her arms around Marisa in a swift, fierce hug and then she was gone.

Marisa walked slowly back to her house, blinking and dabbing at her eyes.

* * *

Louis returned home just after seven. He looked drained and sad even as he swung Sofia up into his arms and put his hand briefly on Marisa's shoulder.

148

'We've made supper,' Marisa said. 'Mainly according to Sofia's instructions — I take the prize for being the world's most disastrous cook.'

Her intention was simply to preserve a veneer of cheeriness to lift the atmosphere of gloom, but Louis was instantly reminded of Diana, light-heartedly regretting her lack of skills in cooking, oblivious to the disaster that was rushing up to destroy their love for each other. He closed his eyes in pain, then slipped back to his own place, splashed cold water on his face and took a bottle of wine from his store.

If it were not for Sofia, he would have been tempted to sit on his own and drink enough so as to obliterate the memory of his most recent image of Poppy: identifying a dead woman, face bloated from being in the water for hours. It was Poppy, all right, but very little to do with the Poppy he used to know.

He had felt curiously empty as he looked at her and afterwards, sitting listlessly on the train as it hurtled south again, he'd had to push away the image of Diana, which kept creeping around the edge of his vision, trying to find a place. On no account must he fantasise about her when he should be thinking of his former wife.

He placed the bottle on the table in Marisa's kitchen and drew the cork. Sofia was watching him with grave, concerned eyes, constantly checking him out as if she wanted to ensure that he was still whole, not about to shatter into little pieces.

'How was school?' he asked her eventually.

'We played some games in the hall and then did maths. And then I went to Miss Peach's group.'

Marisa felt a tiny current of electric feeling spark in the atmosphere. A pulse flickered in Louis' jaw.

'And how did that go?' he asked evenly, taking a sip of wine.

'We did our reading first.' Sofia paused, frowning with the effort of remembering and telling. 'Then I was crying about Mummy, but only for a few minutes.'

Marisa and Louis glanced at each other.

'Miss Peach said just to cry as much as I wanted if I felt sad,' Sofia elaborated. 'And when the others went back to their class, she started crying too.'

Louis laid down his fork.

'I sat on her knee and we both cried,' Sofia said.

Louis laid his forehead against his hand. That night, long after Sofia had fallen asleep, he lay awake through the interminable hours, staring into the dark.

* * *

Diana also found sleep elusive; she had spent the day between hope and despair, unable to believe that Louis would ever look at her again without hatred, then instantly unable to believe that the precious feelings they had shared could be so swiftly and brutally wiped out.

When Sofia had come for her lesson, her pale face so sad, she had thought she would break down completely. She had held onto her self-control like someone clutching at the side of a cliff with their fingertips, just about managing to drag herself through the rest of the school day.

Rupert had left her a voice message. He wanted to come round, to take her out for dinner. 'Angel, I have to see you!' She had been grateful and just a little tempted, but her mind was too full of Louis. She asked him to let her off for that evening, asked him to understand she was not up to it.

He had been superbly understanding, sweet and kind. He didn't deserve rejection, and she agreed to his suggestion to collect her for some diversion on the next evening.

That night had seemed endless as she lay in her bed, praying for sleep to come. After an eternity dawn began to show, stealing into her room and teasing familiar shapes from the dark shadows. She felt her muscles begin to relax, felt herself sliding down into a soft, soporific state . . .

She was walking through a country village. A house beside the road was on fire. A man came running from the smoke. His clothes were smouldering and he was calling for help. Diana reached out her hands but she could do nothing for him.

Then, like a miracle, there was a hose in her hand, cool water gushing. She turned the force of water on the suffering man and the flames licking around him shrivelled and died. She wanted to run towards him to comfort him and soothe his wounds, but she could nothing — her legs were leaden and wayward. She was weeping with despair and frustration and she saw that he was weeping, too.

Louis! Oh, Louis!

153

12

It was now midday on Tuesday; less than forty-eight hours since Poppy's death. Diana summoned up her courage and drove to Louis' house. She knew that she must see him before more time slipped away. Maybe, somehow, something could still be salvaged from the wreckage of Sunday evening.

She felt sick with anxiety as she parked her car, but the moment she stood at the front door she knew that it was deserted; that he had gone. The drumming of her heart slowed. She could see the outline of her figure thrown back at her from the glossy paint as she realised her mission was hopeless. Desolation overtook her and she leaned her head against the painted wood.

A woman's voice startled her. 'He left earlier on. He'll be away for a few days.'

Diana raised her head. The owner of the voice was addressing her across a spiky hedge which divided the two entry paths. She was a tall, striking woman, her dark brown eyes full of life and sympathy — a strange air of knowing.

'Oh,' Diana said, hope finally all dropping away.

'Are you Diana Peach?' the woman asked.

'Yes.'

'I've heard a great deal about you from Sofia. I'm Marisa, the friendly helpful neighbour — at least I hope that's the case,' she said in a dry, self-mocking way.

Diana gave a faint smile. 'Sofia has told me about you, too.'

'Well, as we're so well-acquainted, why don't you come in for a chat? You look as if you could do with a listening ear.'

Diana hesitated, not sure she could cope with a chat. She looked again at the shrewd, sympathetic face and capitulated.

Following Marisa down the hallway, Diana admired the length and slenderness of the older woman's legs, her lean figure shown off in classic black jeans and a cream linen shirt. How old would she be? Diana wondered. Her abundant silver hair wasn't a foolproof indication of age; she had a friend who had gone grey in her twenties.

Marisa took her into the kitchen, a haven of natural waxed woods and the lingering smell of a garlicky supper. Perhaps a supper Louis had shared . . .

'Please, sit down.' Marisa indicated a semi-circular chair of pale oak. She reached for the coffee pot, gently warming on the top of a deep red Aga, and placed it on the table beside two delicate white china cups.

There was something reassuring about this faintly battered, yet elegant room. Diana felt a dog's soft nose nudge her knee and she bent to stroke its silky ears. She recalled Sofia's eager descriptions of a white-muzzled mongrel who was so clever he could almost speak. 'Hello, Risk,' she said to him.

Pouring milk into a jug, Marisa found it impossible not to keep glancing at Diana, bright as a peacock in her lime-green suit and canary-yellow blouse. Her shoes were black suede high heels with tiny bows of yellow at the front.

'Milk, sugar?' she asked her exotic visitor.

'Black, please, no sugar.' Diana's voice was low and attractive, but with no happy lilt of life to it. Marisa saw that she was like a wounded bird — not yet grounded, but definitely struggling. 'Thank you,' she said gratefully as Marisa placed the filled cup in its saucer in front of her.

So this was the fabled Diana Peach, the woman whom Sofia had described so vividly as an adored fairy-tale figure, all lined up to take the place of Mummy. The woman Louis had said very little about, but had clearly also adored.

Marisa was fascinated by Diana's

individual style; the enchanting clothes, and the startling contrast of her dark chestnut hair and pale skin. There was also a haunting, ethereal quality about her which Marisa found particularly intriguing.

'Do you know where Louis has gone?' Diana asked, her voice low and soft.

'Yes. He's gone to New York.'

Diana's eyes flared with feeling: dismay and a stab of alarm.

Marisa wondered whether to elaborate further, but how much did Diana know? Marisa had no idea and when in doubt, it was her policy to keep her mouth shut.

Diana looked down. Her hands trembled when she next lifted her cup.

Marisa sipped her coffee. Louis had talked about not being able to help 'punishing others' two evenings before. It was quite obvious now whom he had been punishing.

'A death causes many ripples,' Marisa observed. 'Especially the violent death of someone still young.'

Diana looked up. 'I've known something was going to happen for weeks. I'm well aware that sounds crazy and unhinged, but I was convinced beyond doubt. Although I never dreamed it would be that — disaster for Poppy.'

Marisa took some time to consider this impassioned statement. 'Then who did you think would be struck down?'

A nerve flickered under Diana's eye. 'It wasn't my fault,' she murmured, partly despairing, partly defiant.

'I think you'll have to help me there,' Marisa said slowly.

'You'll think I'm mad.'

'Maybe we're all a little mad sometimes. I'm prepared to listen — I'll try to understand and not to judge. Truly.'

'I have these dreams,' Diana said. 'I get these pictures in my head about death and dying. They're terrible premonitions, and I know they are going to happen in real life.'

'I see,' Marisa answered slowly.

'Now you do think I'm mad,' Diana said miserably into the growing silence.

'No — in fact I once experienced something similar myself,' Marisa replied evenly. 'A very long time ago.'

Diana gazed at her, startled. 'Do you mean a dream of disaster?' Her tone was cautious.

'My pictures didn't come in the form of dreams,' Marisa explained. 'I saw them when I was awake. And they weren't pictures of disaster as you have experienced. They were images which gave me the ability to predict future happenings in people's lives — a marriage, a move of house or job. That kind of thing.' *Harmless*, thought Marisa, *compared with what Diana was describing*.

Diana glanced at her, checking her sincerity. 'Louis believes one of my dreams is to blame for Poppy's accident. I suppose he thinks that in some strange way I willed it to happen.'

'He's had a terrible shock,' Marisa pointed out. 'He's grieving and feeling guilty and helpless. It's natural, then, to look around for someone to blame. And, don't forget, men tend to be sceptical about the power of the mind. They shy away from that kind of thing, reject it.'

'Yes.' Diana's voice was dull and unconvinced.

'His view will soften in time,' Marisa said gently.

'No,' Diana answered firmly.

'Why do you say that?'

'I can't see a way back to him. I can't see a way through to him. The pictures in my head are clouded in darkness. I can see him in the shadows, and he needs me — but I can't get to him.'

'The pictures could change, given time,' Marisa said.

'I wish I could believe that.'

'The pictures are of your own making,' Marisa pointed out gently. 'And like your conscious thoughts, they too can be shaped and altered as time passes.'

Diana seemed not to be listening. 'He loved me so much,' she said sadly. 'It was a true, deep love, even though we've only known each other a short time. And now he hates me. In the pictures in his head I'm nothing more than Poppy's murderer.'

'No,' Marisa said very softly.

'My mother used to go to Tarot readings,' she told Marisa. 'Once a year in January. She had complete faith in the readings and believed everything she was told, the poor darling, even when things hadn't come true from the last year's reading.'

'Did anything from the readings come true?'

'One or two things. They always told her she would be travelling a great deal and have minor problems with her health.'

'Go on.'

Diana smiled — it was the first time she had smiled properly since entering the house. 'My mother always took several holidays a year, and she was something of a hypochondriac. It wasn't surprising that the cards got those things right.'

'So, were you a sceptic?'

'No, I was open-minded,' Diana said.

'Maybe it's only those who are truly open-minded who can receive premonitions such as yours,' Marisa observed. 'Is your mother still alive?'

'No.' Diana was startled. 'Why do you ask?'

'I was simply interested. How did she die?'

Diana hesitated, wondering how much to reveal. 'She was killed in a car crash. She saw a magpie flying towards her in the garden — a terrible omen — and then she went out in her car and was crushed by a tractor.'

Marisa said nothing.

'I wish these dreams would leave me alone!' Diana exclaimed. 'I have to live again. Even if I've lost Louis, I must have some life back.' The passion in her voice was almost ferocious.

'You must have hope,' Marisa said softly.

'About Louis?' Diana said sharply. 'You didn't see his face when he received the news. Something in him was dying — and it was his love for me.'

She got up. 'I have to go now. I'll be late for my afternoon teaching session.'

Marisa watched Diana get into her car, a firm, set look on her face. She had the look of someone resigned to their fate; someone who would be stoic and patient in the face of the tyranny of destiny.

13

Rupert was waiting on the doorstep when Diana got home from work. He gave her a hug and kissed the crown of her head, which was all she was prepared to submit to for now.

He had recognised that it would take time to wean her from her state of lovesickness and banish Louis Rogier from her thoughts. He judged himself up to the challenge. In fact, her loyalty to the other man rather impressed him, made him keener than ever.

She walked ahead of him into the house, picking up the mail, and leading the way through to the sitting room. 'I'll make us some tea,' she said, a shade too formally for his liking.

'A G-and-T would be nice,' he remarked.

'Help yourself,' she invited him, indicating the drinks cabinet. 'I'll just go and freshen up a little.'

'Don't be too long,' he warned, teasing and tender.

Locking herself in the bathroom, she scanned through the mail and — oh joy — there was something from Louis. Just glancing at his handwriting with its long, strong strokes made her faint with longing. The paper shook in her unsteady fingers as she unfolded it.

My dear Diana

I am flying Poppy's body back to New York. I thought it best not to come and tell you my plans. You will understand why.

I think you will know, too, that there are many things we should have said to each other, but perhaps these are things it would be best to leave unsaid.

Louis

Diana stared at the words. So formal, so cold. Words of a final farewell with no glimmer of hope. Despair overwhelmed her. Her legs were weak and trembling. *I'm falling apart*, she whispered to herself in horror.

Beyond the locked door she heard footsteps, the crackle of a newspaper, the fizz of a cap being released from a bottle of tonic. She reminded herself of the here and now. Reality. Rupert.

She straightened her spine and breathed deeply. Her hand tightened on the paper she still held until it buckled and shrank into a ball, warm and damp from the heat of her hand.

A calm stillness came over her. She brushed her hair and stroked fragrance on the pulse points of her skin. Holding herself steady, she returned to the sitting room.

Rupert glanced up. 'More gorgeous than ever.' He patted the space beside him. Diana sat down, making herself put the image of Louis from her mind and give Rupert her full attention.

'I want to take you for a drive in the country,' he announced.

'What, now?'

'Yup.'

To meet his parents, she thought with sudden intuition.

'I'd like to show you off to Rupert senior and my mother,' he said, grinning. 'Come on — they're expecting us.'

★　★　★

In the car she said, 'I'm very happy to meet your parents. I never had a proper family — I like the whole idea of families — but I'm not prepared to be shown off like a trophy.'

'Ouch! I keep forgetting you're not a girl to be trifled with.'

'And I'm not a girl,' she pointed out.

'Sorry, sorry. A figure of speech.'

'Forgiven.' Tentatively she touched the back of his hand with fleeting fingertips.

They left the urban sprawl of London and were soon passing through wooded terrain interspersed with walled parkland.

Diana became increasingly curious to know what she would find at the end of the journey. She really knew very little about Rupert, apart from his seemingly part-time job in a merchant bank and his interest in horses. She knew that he lived in a small flat in Chelsea when he was in London. But he had not really spoken of his parents at all. And being taken up with Louis, she had not bothered to enquire further.

Rupert took the car through some tall iron gates. There was a long, straight drive leading up to a substantial house built of grey stone. A country house; a small stately home.

'The original building dates from the time of Queen Anne,' Rupert commented. 'It's been extended once or twice since then.' He said all this quite casually, but she could tell he was deeply proud of the family house. 'It's called Percival,' he added. 'After some ancestor or other — Ma knows the history, I'm utterly hopeless with all that kind of thing.'

'It's beautiful,' breathed Diana. She and her mother had always lived in large, comfortable houses with antiques and silk drapes, but this was different: a house of history and lineage.

'I thought you'd like it,' Rupert said with satisfaction. He offered his hand to help her out of the car. 'You look beautiful,' he commented admiringly. 'Like a mysterious queen in an old Egyptian painting.'

'I thought history wasn't your strong point,' she said drily.

Rupert Pym senior turned out to be an older, rangier version of his son; his once blond hair was now a creamy white mane. Wearing baggy corduroys and an old, hairy sweater, he came forward to meet Diana with intense curiosity in his face.

Rupert was all delighted exuberance. 'Pa, this is Diana, the elusive maiden I've told you so much about.'

Diana felt her hand clasped briefly and then released. 'Good journey?' Mr Pym asked politely. 'Rupert keep to the speed limit, did he? He can be a bit of a demon behind the wheel.'

Diana smiled. 'Some of the time.'

She looked around the hall, admiring the high arched and latticed windows, the great oak staircase branching into two halfway up and leading to a graceful carved gallery.

'Where's Ma?' Rupert enquired.

'Somewhere in the garden, where else?'

'Ma is devoted to the soil and her plants,' Rupert told Diana.

'Indeed she is, I hardly ever see her.' Rupert's father was still observing Diana, making no attempt to disguise his continuing curiosity. She looked him straight in the eye and gave an enigmatic smile.

'You're going to have to change into something more practical, Diana,' Rupert's father informed her. 'My wife will have you grubbing about in the greenhouses, showing you what's what before you can say marsh marigold. And I must warn you she has two frightfully undisciplined Labradors who will wreck that delightful outfit of yours in two minutes flat.'

'I see I've been cast in the role of the little town girl woefully ill-equipped for the rigours of the country,' Diana said with a smile of mischief. 'Perhaps you could loan me an all-enveloping mackintosh and some green wellies?

'That's the spirit!' Rupert's father patted her shoulder in a congratulatory fashion as though she had cleared some sort of hurdle. 'I'll dig something out right away.'

'You see,' Rupert told his parent. 'A girl of spirit and wit. What did I tell you? She's a miracle.'

* * *

Later on, dinner was served in a large hushed dining room. Rupert and his father were both natural conversationalists, allowing for no awkward pauses. His mother, joining them a little late and rather breathless, was friendly and brisk. Around sixty, she struck Diana as a woman who would have been a country belle in her youth, but was now somewhat ruddy and weathered from being continually outdoors. She was wearing a blue dress of figured brocade which reminded Diana of those her mother had worn when she was a child. Any glamorous effect was ruined however by the sagging, bobbled beige cardigan Mrs Pym had put on over the dress, in defence of the deep chill of the Percival dining-room even in early summer.

'You're a teacher, I hear,' Rupert's mother said to Diana in a blunt, down-to-earth manner. It sounded like a faint challenge.

'I teach English as a second language to young children.'

'And are there many who need that kind of teaching?' Rupert's mother asked. 'Children of school age who know no English?'

'Quite a few,' Diana answered, smiling.

'She's not really a career girl,' Rupert cut in, reaching for the wine and topping up his glass.

Diana turned to him. 'What makes you say that?'

'Because, angel, I've been out with a few girls who certainly were. And you're not one jot like them.'

Diana looked at him with fresh interest. He had a point.

She had always liked her job, she liked the challenge of motivating the children and she loved their company, but she had no ambition for climbing the promotion ladder. She recognised, too, that her job was something of a hobby, something to interest her and provide a focus for the days, because there had never been any need for her to make money.

Her ambitions were directed elsewhere — in her heart and her spirit. At the back of her mind there had always been the image of perfect love, of a passionate and deeply solid marriage, of children . . .

Her mind flew to Sofia. If she had any responsibility for the love and care of Sofia, she knew the job would be pushed very firmly into second place. *Oh, Sofia, Louis!*

'More wine, darling?' Rupert put his hand on hers and prised her wine glass from her fingers. He glanced into her face. 'Angel! Are you all right?'

She realised she had been clutching the fat stem of her wine glass so tightly that the chiselled cuts had left red weals on her skin. She smiled at him. 'Yes — I'm perfectly fine, Rupert.' She felt a rush of affection for him. He seemed to have a knack of stepping in when she needed comfort and solace.

'I never wanted a career,' Rupert's mother remarked. 'I never wanted anything except a husband and children, a quiet country life, and a garden.'

'Mentioned last, but rating no means least,' Rupert quipped.

'And,' Mrs Pym continued, fixing Diana with a stern eye, 'I have always been terribly proud of my husband's career. When a man has the responsibility of sitting on the board of several international companies, I believe he would prefer his wife not to be out there in the world competing. Men like a little female nurturing and support, whatever they tell you in the media, even in these modern times.'

Diana smiled diplomatically. All this was so familiar, just the kind of conversation that used to go on at her mother's little supper parties. She wondered what Louis' view would be. She felt a huge stab of longing at the thought of discussing the issue with him. His ideas were always so well thought-out and clear, and never prejudiced. Except on one issue.

She took a long drink of wine. *Stop thinking of him!* The pain was flaring up all over again and she drove it back.

'What do you think, Rupert?' she asked him softly.

'What? Oh! About women working . . . ' He grinned. 'I always support my mama — it wouldn't do to argue with her at her own dinner table.'

'I admire the kind of work you're doing,' Rupert's father put in. 'I would imagine the children you work with are not the easiest to handle.'

'I suppose not,' Diana agreed, looking at the older man with new interest. 'But I've found that children are usually co-operative if you can just find the right way to gain their interest.'

'Keep the little devils busy?'

'Exactly.' She smiled.

'We've never found the secret of keeping this little devil busy,' he continued wryly, looking pointedly at his son.

'Too busy playing instead,' his mother said with brutal frankness and obvious affection. 'Usually with leggy blondes.'

'True,' Rupert admitted, unabashed. 'I rather fancy I'm becoming a changed man, though.' He gave the chestnut-haired Diana a long, lingering look.

At the end of the dinner, Rupert's mother escorted Diana to the drawing room, leaving the two men to get out the port.

'We're very traditional here,' she told Diana with peppery irony. 'I expect you'll have noticed.' Diana smiled and her hostess continued, 'I like tradition. I like the progress of the seasons, the rhythm of my garden here at Percival.' She looked at Diana. 'Do you think you could learn to like all that, too?'

'Are you asking me if I could live here at Percival?' Diana stared at her.

'Yes. I like you,' Rupert's mother announced. 'You're rather different to the young women he's brought here before.'

'How so?' Diana asked.

'More grown up,' Rupert's mother answered eventually. 'And you have more . . . depth. I'm afraid that Rupert is rather a pup still, although he has a good heart and would never knowingly hurt anyone.' She paused. 'He needs responsibilities to make a man of him,' she said with feeling.

'I see,' Diana said.

'Yes, I rather think you do.' Rupert's mother stood up abruptly and crossed to the drinks tray set on a table by the window. 'Do you enjoy liqueurs? I have some rather nice ones I brought back from Tuscany last autumn. Now tell me about your family, your parents. Is your father in the City? What committees does your mother sit on?'

Diana smiled to herself. Being at Percival was like stepping back into another century.

'I think I've been given the full parental scrutiny,' Diana told Rupert as they walked around the garden at dusk. 'What did you tell them about me?'

'Hardly a thing. Well, let's face it, what do I know about you, my angel? You're a simply delicious mystery.'

'Your mother was very frank. In fact I almost expected to be asked if I had good child-bearing hips.'

'Ah yes. The gateway for the son and heir to Percival. The poor parents are getting desperate. And do you, angel?'

'Have child-bearing hips?' She shrugged. 'I wouldn't know.'

'We can't go back to London tonight, sweetheart,' he said, pressing her against him. 'I'm over the limit, not fit to drive.'

And I'm over the limit too, thought Diana. Rupert had made sure of that. 'I need to be in school for eleven tomorrow morning,' she said with a touch of sharpness.

'You will be, darling, you will! So, you'll stay the night?'

'Thank you. That's very kind.'

He turned her towards him, tipped her face up and put his lips on hers. Diana felt warm breath, the contact of another human being. Nothing else. *Too soon*, she told herself.

'Rupert, I'm not going to sleep with you,' she told him.

'Angel! I wouldn't have dreamed of presuming,' he protested. But both of them knew it was a lie.

They walked back to the house and parted in the hall. Diana made her way up to the guest room in the west wing under the guidance of Rupert's mother.

The room looked like something from a period drama. The furniture was all fashioned gleaming mahogany and the bed was a four-poster, curtained in heavy paisley silk.

She lay beneath the covers, reviewing

the events of the evening. It struck her that all the correct formalities leading to an alliance had been set in motion by Rupert's parents — rather like something out of a Jane Austen novel — and Rupert seemed to be playing the game with a will.

It was all entirely the opposite of what had happened between her and Louis; that instant knowledge that they were twin souls. *Don't think of it!* With tears swelling in her throat and utterly exhausted from the effort of keeping up a brave front, she slid down swiftly into a deep sleep. There were no dreams.

14

'Louis — I'm so sorry to hear the terrible news.' Mary Cartland was shaken. 'I really hadn't expected anything like this.'

'I'd have thought you'd have seen it coming,' Louis responded. He smiled, his eyes not unfriendly, but detached.

He never gives anything away, Mary thought. She spread out the pictures he had given her for inspection. 'These are brilliant, Louis. They are simply fantastic.'

She was looking at recent shots of a household-name TV presenter. In her minimally stylish loft apartment, impeccably made up, blow-dried, and casually beautiful in a silk shirt and designer jeans, she radiated glamour, success and confidence.

That was what you saw when you first looked at the shots. But when you looked again you could see that, in some curious way, Louis had gradually peeled away the woman's outer coating of triumphant complacency and captured a trace of self-doubt. It was that tiny hint of vulnerability that made the shots so intriguingly appealing.

'What can I say, except stunning?' Mary swung round to face him. 'So this is it, the last celebrity shoot. Never again!'

'Never say never,' Louis quipped.

'So what will you do?'

He raised his shoulders. The enigmatic smile came again.

'The Gallic shrug!' Mary exclaimed. 'You don't fool me, Louis. I'll bet you know exactly what you're going to do next.'

'In truth, Mary, no — I don't.'

She assessed him through narrowed eyes. He was lean and tanned from the hot summer and his face had strangely beautiful lines of grief etched around his mouth. She caught herself wallowing in adolescent-style yearning. 'I'm talking about life,' she said, 'not work.'

'You're a very perceptive woman, Mary,' he responded. 'I have some plans to do some shoots in Leeds and Durham, taking post-war developments as a theme.'

'Do you have a commission?'

He shook his head slowly. 'Not yet,' he said.

'Brave,' she commented. 'Or fool-hardy.'

'Maybe.' He went to the window and looked at his favourite view along the docks to the Dartford Bridge. He drummed on the glass — a soft but urgent rhythm.

'You know,' he told Mary, 'when I went to New York to take Poppy's body back to Liam, I found I really liked the guy. I'd thought the visit would be a nightmare, but it wasn't. He was very generous, insisting on giving me the paintings she had in the gallery. I've sold quite a few already.' He threw her a sardonic glance. 'So the wolf isn't quite at the door yet.'

'Good.'

'I've discovered a couple of really promising artists up in the north and I've managed to squeeze some funds out of various organisations to help them out while they're working on new projects. I'm seriously thinking of setting up a gallery.'

Mary could see that the chances of more celebrity shoots from Louis' camera were pretty remote. She was sorry on her own behalf, but glad for him that he was building alternatives.

'How's Sofia?' she asked.

'She's fine. She likes school and she has some good friends.' The drumming had slowed whilst he talked of his new projects; now it sped up again, restless and insistent.

When he left, Mary sent up a silent but heartfelt prayer to whatever deity might be around to hear, asking for Louis to fill the emptiness and loss which was surely eating into his heart.

★ ★ ★

Louis took the Tube going west. After two stops, he got off and walked along the road in which Diana's house stood.

Autumn was throwing a mantle of wistful bronze and gold over the leaves on the trees. The sun glinted on the polished windows of the elegant houses.

The image of Diana constantly lingered in his senses. He felt a simple need just to be in the street where she lived.

At first, his shock and confusion at Poppy's death had prompted him to blame someone, and he had directed the stream of his cold anger on to Diana alone. And because of her intense belief in the power of her dreams, which was something alien and unknown to him, he had been able to sustain his disdain and fury over a number of weeks.

When cool reason came softly seeping back, the anger had begun to dissipate. He began to see things differently. He had looked through all his photographs of Poppy and stared at them with curiosity and old, dead love, and he had also examined photos Liam had taken of her the day before the crash, giving several to Louis to have as a keepsake.

Louis scoured the picture for clues, of some sign that Poppy herself had had some intimation of the tragedy which would end her life, but he could find nothing. She gazed back at him, a confident, successful young woman looking forward to the new life she had manufactured for herself. Maybe that confidence was the fundamental difference between Poppy and Diana. The one supremely sure of herself; the other pricked by doubts, but gifted with a certain strange conviction which she was brave enough to share.

When he recalled the raw cruelty with which he had thrust Diana from him, he shuddered with self-disgust. He felt unworthy to approach her again, for he'd been totally rejecting.

As a father, he felt himself to be doing rather better. And through the summer he and Sofia had begun to shape a new life for themselves. Sofia had gradually lapsed into silence about Diana once the school term ended. Just once, she had asked Louis when Diana was going to come again for supper and he had told her that he didn't know, and he thought that perhaps he and Diana couldn't be friends any more. In a child's instinctive way, Sofia had understood what was necessary. She had not asked any further questions, but Louis guessed she was biding her time and silently hoping.

Approaching Diana's house, he slowed his pace. The *For Sale* sign swung gently in the light breeze. It had been in place for weeks now. He wondered how many interested prospective buyers had been to view the property.

He knew all about the swerve in her life plans. Her engagement to Rupert Pym, announced in The Times, had been accompanied by an attractive photograph and an informative piece on the couple's plans. A wedding was to take place in the spring. Renovations were in progress at the family residence, Percival, in preparation for the couple to take over the main wing of the house after their marriage.

Louis had read all this with grim fascination. *A honeymoon on some exotic and exclusive island,* he had added to himself; *the patter of a little heir's feet some time in the year following.*

He forced himself not to stop in front of her house. An image of Diana in Rupert's embrace rose up to taunt him. The pain of loss and the pain of wanting her stabbed at him without mercy.

15

A few weeks following their engagement, Rupert bought Diana a puppy; a red setter with ridiculously long ears and an even longer pedigree.

'Got to get her into the way of being a country girl,' he joked. Sometimes when he caught a glimpse of her talking to his mother in the garden, wearing one of her vividly coloured outfits that marked her out as special, he felt a jolt of unease. By the side of his amiable, sturdy mother, Diana was an exotic bird of paradise. Rupert was infatuated with her — she was utterly gorgeous and so different from the hearty, horse-mad girls living on neighbouring estates. He loved showing her off at the country set's dinner parties — her delicate charm, her wit, her sense of style — but would she ever manage to fit in?

He knew that his parents liked her and that they were overjoyed to see him 'settling down' at last, but he was pretty sure they were starting to have worries too. There was some quality of Diana that eluded their understanding. Rupert had decided it was her delicate physique and seeming fragility that concerned them. But for himself, it was the vibes she gave off of purity of mind and spirit that were a bit bothersome. Charming, of course, and unique in his experience, but maybe she was little *too* pure and spirit-like — and maybe a dog was just the thing to move her on to matters more ... sensual. As far as Rupert was concerned, a dog was a symbol of earthiness, of country living and damp walks over carpets of rotting leaves.

He told her nothing of his plan. Early one Saturday morning, at the start of a full weekend of social engagements at Percival, he slipped out to a breeder he had contacted earlier and collected the eight-week-old puppy he had ordered.

Although he had been brought up with dogs and been used to them always being around, he had never had the responsibility of the actual care of an animal; that side of things was dealt with by his mother or her staff. Rupert would occasionally take the dogs for walks if he felt in the mood and hurl sticks for them to chase. In the evenings he liked to see them lying by the fire.

It was a long time since there had been a puppy at Percival and Rupert had forgotten how primitive and wayward they were — a mixture of unbridled energy and very little sense. This particular specimen was all piston-like legs and fizzing enthusiasm for life. Once in the car, it refused to sit still for a moment; in the end he had to force it down against the seat by the scruff of its neck and drive with one hand.

Scooping the animal up into his arms when they arrived back at Percival, he ran easily up the stairs, bound for Diana's room in the west wing. Grappling with the elastically squirming puppy in his arms, he knocked sharply on the door.

Waiting for some answer from within, Rupert was jarringly reminded of the curiousness of his relationship with Diana. A few months before, he would never have believed such a set-up possible. They had been engaged for some weeks now, there had been announcements in all the quality papers, a solitaire diamond to seal the bond, and a big celebration party at Percival . . . and still he did not feel that he was permitted to intrude on Diana's privacy in her bedroom or bathroom.

He sometimes saw himself in the position of his father, who he had often mocked for standing tapping tentatively on his mother's door, calling out gruffly, 'Are you decent?'

Diana opened the door and stood looking at him. She was barefoot, simply dressed in dark blue jeans and a cream silk shirt. Her hair was newly washed, gleaming around her pale face. She looked at the puppy; she looked up at Rupert.

'A present for you, darling,' he said.

Diana put out her hand and touched the puppy's ears. 'Oh goodness!' she said.

'Well, what do you think?'

'She's beautiful.'

'How did you know it's a bitch?' Rupert demanded.

Diana shrugged, smiling. 'I can't say. I felt she was a she.'

The puppy was wriggling like fury now, panicking to be set down and let free.

Rupert dropped her lightly to the floor and she immediately dashed into Diana's room and squatted on the carpet. A small shiny puddle appeared, growing to the size of a tea plate.

Rupert strode into the room, grabbed the puppy by the neck and rubbed its nose in the mess it had made.

'No!' Diana exclaimed, wrenching Rupert's hand away from the quivering puppy. She wrenched it with a strength that surprised him. '*No!*'

He stared at her and laughed.

'Animals have to learn the hard way. They soon get to know the difference between right and wrong.'

Diana gave him a level stare which made him take a small step backwards. There was just the odd occasion when he glimpsed something behind her gentle façade which rather concerned him — the look in her eyes was a touch scary.

'You have to be a little cruel to be kind,' he volunteered. 'Come on, darling, stop looking at me as if *I'm* the one who's just made a mess on the carpet!'

Diana sat on the floor. The puppy gambolled up to her and put its paws on her chest, making putty-coloured paw marks on the cream silk. She laid her hand on the puppy's long, delicate neck and stroked it with a tenderness that made Rupert ferociously jealous. 'Animals learn by encouragement and praise,' she said quietly. 'And kindness.'

'For heaven's sake, Diana, I was hardly brutal.'

She looked up at him again and he

felt that he had made some terrible mistake, revealed to her a facet of himself that perhaps should have been kept secret.

He looked down at the puppy, nestling close against Diana's breasts — an intimacy which he, her fiancé, had not so far been permitted. Damn dog — he wished he'd never dreamed up the whole daft scheme of getting an animal for Diana. He could see nothing but trouble ahead.

'I think she's hungry,' Diana said, tickling the puppy's ears as it nuzzled against her.

'Well, it won't get much joy there, will it?' Rupert remarked with sarcasm, staring at the swell of Diana's breasts.

'Hardly.' Diana laughed. 'Poor little thing,' she said to the puppy, her voice warm and tender, 'you've only just left your mother, haven't you?'

Good grief! thought Rupert. *This puppy's going to get more tender loving care than me.*

'What does she eat?' Diana enquired.

Rupert was well and truly caught out. He smiled appealingly, like a naughty little boy. 'God only knows. Oh dear!'

'I'll go prepare her some warm milk,' Diana decided, standing up with the puppy still cuddled against her. 'And then I'll drive into the village and get whatever else she needs.'

Rupert watched her walk towards the staircase, small, slender and exquisite. He loved her physical fragility and the way it contrasted with the strangely steely detachment in her personality; she seemed as unfathomable as when he had first met her. It often struck him that, while he had captured her, he in no way possessed her — yet. He sat on her bed, pondering. How much longer was she going to make him wait?

She came back after a while, the puppy cradled in her arms and looking drowsy. Diana smiled down at her, wiping the lacing of milk from her soft puppy lips with a gentle finger. She laid the puppy on the bed, and stroked it softly. Soon it was asleep.

Rupert was reminded forcefully of the sleeping arrangements of his parents. How his mother's pongy Labradors snored the night away on her bed while his father slept alone in the room next door.

He looked at Diana, desperately desirable and somehow eternally unattainable. *Things are going to change,* he told himself. He stepped up close to her. She looked up and smiled.

'Thank you, Rupert,' she said simply.

'You like the puppy?'

'Oh yes.'

'Are you sure? You know I'm a bit of a blunderer sometimes.'

'I'm sure that I like her.' Diana smiled.

'Do I get a reward?'

There was a long, silent pause and then she stood up, put her arms around his waist and laid her head against his chest. Rupert stroked her neck, the flesh beneath his fingers felt like heavy silk. 'Diana, do you love me?' he asked.

She said nothing, her hands moving

along his spine, exploring him in a way she had never done before. She raised her head and parted her lips.

Rupert decided this must be her answer. He wrapped her tightly in his arms and pressed his lips against hers. After some moments she pulled back a little.

'Do you love me?' she asked him, softly.

'Angel, I don't think I've ever wanted a woman so much in my whole life,' he breathed.

Her body was still resting against him. Tentatively he stroked her collar bones, then allowed his fingers to move downwards. Softly, and oh so slowly, he made contact with the V-shaped divide of her shirt.

Diana's eyes were still closed, her features unreadable.

'Angel!' he exclaimed. 'Have pity! I've been living the life of a monk, you know.'

'I know.' She spoke very softly. 'And I'm sorry.'

And then the reality of the situation suddenly hit her like a swung plank of wood. Her brain reeled as an image of Louis' face rose up to fill her vision. She saw his dark eyes full of hurt and deep reproach. She stiffened, tensing like an animal and pulled away from Rupert.

No, no, no! an inner voice screamed.

At that moment the puppy raised its head, letting out a volley of high-pitched barks as footsteps approached down the corridor and there was a sharp rap on the door.

'Rupert!' came his mother's low but imperious voice. 'Rupert, are you there? Your old school chum, Ben, has just called. He'd like to see you. I've been calling and calling you.'

Rupert swore under his breath. 'Bloody b-word damn, damn, damn!' He smiled ruefully at Diana. 'Angel, I'll have to leave you for a moment. When Mama calls, one must obey!' He gave her a wicked wink. 'Don't run away.'

Diana stared at him, amazed. He had

no idea of the turmoil she felt inside. No inkling that he had been about to be well and truly repulsed. As he slipped through the door, she was not sure whether to be grateful or sorry to have been spared the drama of a confrontation. She felt a stab of panic and confusion regarding the near future, a sense of having trapped herself in a locked cage. She tried to offer herself rational explanations for the powerful repulsion she had felt anticipating sex with Rupert. She told herself it was simply too soon, she was not ready to give herself yet. She knew she would not feel ready until they were married. Within marriage, sex was proper and dignified, but even then . . .

Willing herself to be convinced, she got changed and lifted her puppy into her arms. She would take the young dog out into the garden to show to Rupert's mother, knowing that in the company of that redoubtable lady she, Diana, would be utterly safe from any further amorous advances.

There was a dinner party for twelve in the Percival dining room that evening. The old rules of the English upper class still prevailed there. The men were in black tie and the women wore low-cut evening frocks. The table was polished to mirror-like brilliance and an ornate crested dinner-service set out. Flames from the burning logs in the great marble fireplace glinted on the delicate Georgian silver cutlery.

Rupert's mother had insisted on Diana and Rupert taking the host and hostess's places at the head and foot of the table, making no secret of her plan to groom them in readiness for their eventual role as master and mistress of Percival.

Diana, a delicate glowing figure in bright scarlet with black and silver jewellery, smiled hesitantly at her fiancé across several feet of mahogany. He raised his glass and blew her a kiss. He was on splendid form, cracking jokes and taking full advantage of his father's excellent claret and the Muscat which was served to accompany the pudding.

Diana picked at the pheasant on her plate. It looked overcooked and unappetising. Rupert's mother liked her food to be plain and simple and the cook was instructed accordingly. The meat was curled up at the edges, as dry as a stick, and served with 'game chips' which Diana guessed were probably crisps from a packet.

She took a sip of wine and had a sudden memory of Louis' delicious and imaginative cooking. The mere sound of his name in her head made her momentarily dizzy with longing. *Don't think of him!* she told herself. *Don't, don't!*

She tried to catch Rupert's eye but he was leaning across to the woman on his left, entertaining her with one of his racy stories. Diana watched him for a few minutes.

Rupert is basically a good and decent man, she told herself fiercely, fresh panic rising in her throat at the thought of the future. She laid down her cutlery and her napkin, got up and walked around the table. Dropping a light kiss on Rupert's head she excused herself and went through the kitchen into the utility room where the puppy lay dozing on a pile of old coats beside the door.

The cook, painstakingly putting the final touches on a large sherry trifle, smiled as she entered.

'Sweet little thing,' she said, nodding towards the puppy. 'I had to put her out while I cut the birds up. She's not too young to know what a good roast is.'

The puppy came suddenly to life, gambolled up to Diana and scrabbled at her leg, creating an instant ladder in her glossy black stocking. She then shook her ears with a great flap and gazed lovingly at her new mistress. Diana scooped her up and took her into the garden. She watched the puppy inhale the earthy evening scents of the garden and patter about, poking her nose in the bushes. Diana waited patiently, enjoying the sensation of drinking in the fresh damp air. She felt as though she had been sprung from some kind of captivity.

'Good girl!' she told the puppy when eventually the desired performance was completed. She gathered the warm furry body into her arms and took her inside. She wondered what to call her. Rupert had suggested something noble like Circe or Miranda. Diana did not think so. What name, then? She didn't know. She didn't see to be able to make even the simplest decision at the moment. Not since she had said 'yes' when Rupert asked her to marry him.

How could that have happened? she asked herself. How could she have let events and fate simply roll over her?

Hugging her dog close, she could feel its heart beating, rapid and urgent. A surge of love for the small creature welled up inside her. 'I am starving for love,' she whispered in sudden, terrible understanding.

She recalled the events of that morning. Rupert had touched her very gently, very skilfully, but he had not moved her, and for a few moments of madness she had stood on the brink of betraying the only man she had ever loved.

She put the puppy to bed near the still-warm oven and then returned to the ritual of the extended dinner party in the Percival dining room. Taking her place opposite Rupert, she leaned towards the guests to her left and right, noting if they required more wine, asking if they had enjoyed their dinner, if they wanted anything further.

No one detected any sign of her inner turmoil; her public mask was quite perfect.

★　★　★

When the guests had all gone, she went to her room and splashed cold water on her face. Returning to the ground floor, she found the place already in darkness.

Creeping into the drawing room, she found Rupert stretched out on one of the sofas snoring softly. She placed tentative fingers on his forehead.

'A little far gone,' he murmured sleepily. 'No damn good for anything, angel. Be fine in the morning.'

Her heart singing with relief, she made her way back to the kitchen where her puppy was sound asleep, totally blissful. Diana smiled. Her eyes moved to the phone on the wall, placed there for the benefit of the staff in the era before the mobile phone. It was still in use, there being a poor, almost non-existent signal for cell phones at Percival.

She lifted the receiver and her heart accelerated as her fingers tapped out the familiar number sequence, long-neglected because she had not trusted herself to use it. As a connection was established and the rhythmic purrs began, she felt herself move into another sphere; begin to live on a different plane.

His voice sounded in her ear. 'Hello,

yes?' Low and sensual, rich with sensitivity, and very male.

Louis.

Diana drew in a long breath. She found herself transfixed, unable to speak. That he was still alive, still there for her, still him, made her want to howl out loud like an animal.

'Diana! Darling!' His understanding was instant, his tone filled with urgency. 'It is you, isn't it?'

She swallowed. Her voice died in her throat.

'Diana, listen to me, it's all right, darling. Talk to me — say something, please!'

'I shouldn't be doing this,' she murmured.

He began to speak in French. 'Don't hang up, Diana. Stay with me, let talk to you, my darling!'

Diana found tears filling her eyes, dazzling her with a curtain of silvery liquid. He was no longer angry; he loved her again. He had always loved her. She understood all of that now

— but it was too late.

'You don't have to speak, just listen. I was a fool, I hurt you terribly. I've been crazy with worry, wondering how you were.'

'Yes,' she breathed softly, tuning into his thoughts, knowing that his feelings mirrored hers.

'I've been giving myself hell, thinking of you hurting as badly as I've been.'

'Louis,' she breathed. Simply saying his name was a precious luxury, as though she were caressing him, tracing her fingers over the beautiful bones of his face.

'I've been going out of my mind, racking my brains for a means of finding my way back to you.' He paused. 'Say something, Diana! For God's sake!'

'I never blamed you,' she managed at last.

'I was in shock, raging and hitting out. Do you forgive me? Do you still love me?'

'Yes!' Ah, the simple relief of simply speaking the truth. 'Of course I do.'

She heard his sharp intake of breath. 'Then let me come for you — now! Tell me where you are.'

She sighed despairingly.

'Diana!' His voice was suddenly hard and insistent. 'Are you with him — Rupert?'

'I'm staying with his family for a while,' she said carefully. 'They hosted a dinner party tonight and Rupert's . . . a bit the worse for wear.'

'So we can talk freely?'

For a few moments she could not speak at all. 'Not really, Louis. I'm sorry.'

'Darling, don't do this to me,' Louis protested. 'Don't slip away from me again. I couldn't bear it.'

Diana lifted the receiver away from her ear and stared at it as though it held a secret she had been desperately seeking but unable to find. She had an unshakable conviction that the link which had been so cruelly broken between her and Louis was now whole again. A miraculous reconnection had been made. And that must be enough. There was nothing else she could say.

'There's something else, isn't there?' he said slowly, with his disturbing intuition.

'Yes.'

'You can tell me,' he said. 'Anything, darling, anything. You can trust me.'

'No,' she said, in a whisper.

Fighting back her distress, feeling that she was plunging a rapier into her heart, she gently replaced the receiver.

His voice echoed in the silence.

16

Louis couldn't sleep. His thoughts, constantly winging to Diana, whirled around his brain, all finishing up in frustrating dead ends, but by the time the light eventually crept into the sky, he knew that he had to find some way to help her. Help her deal with the dreams coming from her unconscious, and help her to leave Rupert and come back to him. Just how that would be achieved he hadn't yet worked out.

He took Sofia to school and then went into central London to buy further stationery for printing out photographs. While walking down Oxford Street his glance was drawn to a display in the window of a bookshop — a double row of hardback books titled *Unlocking the Secrets of the Mind* by Professor Edward Penrose.

Walking into the shop, he saw that a

signing session was in progress. A middle-aged man sat behind a table piled with further copies of the book he had seen in the window. He was big and rather rumpled and frayed-looking, his hair a wilful mop of steely grey. He had the look of an academic, crossed with an elderly superstar, and his grey eyes were like razors. It was obvious to Louis that this man was Professor Penrose.

Looking on for a while, Louis saw that the professor was doing brisk business, signing and selling his book. He was also happy to talk with the customers, and the whole session seemed to be buzzing with energy and excitement.

Intrigued and curiously hopeful, Louis joined the queue. It took quite a time to get to the front and meet Penrose, but Louis was happy to wait. Having purchased a copy of the book, he watched the professor inscribe a dedication.

'Can we talk later?' Louis asked Penrose as he closed the book and passed it over to him. 'When you're through here?'

It was a naked and bold request, but Louis didn't care. He had a feeling that this man might be the one to give him some clue on how to help Diana. The professor looked up, his sharp grey eyes instantly filling with shrewd speculation. 'Sure. Just hang around for a few more minutes and we'll meet up again.'

An hour went by before the professor had no choice but to call it a day, the book having completely sold out, including the window display copies. He chatted for a few minutes to the bookshop manager, then eventually made his way over to Louis who had been browsing through the photography section.

Louis extended his hand. 'I'm Louis Rogier. Thanks for agreeing to talk to me.'

Penrose shook his hand vigorously. 'You look like a man who wants answers to some questions,' he commented astutely and without preamble.

Louis nodded and smiled. 'You're

right. Can I buy you a drink some-where? Lunch, perhaps?'

Penrose beamed. 'What a splendid idea. The perfect time. And far better than going home to my lonely flat.'

Louis took the professor to a little basement brasserie where they settled down with a bottle of red and a seafood platter.

The professor took a long slug of wine. 'Well, now,' he said, getting straight down to the nitty-gritty, 'this is all very intriguing. Tell me what I can help you with.'

'I'm hopelessly in love with a very lovely and wonderful woman,' Louis said, intuitively knowing that Penrose was a man to be absolutely straight with and probably one who did not suffer fools and time-wasters gladly.

'You French guys, so romantic,' Penrose commented drily.

'Perhaps, but I've managed to make a total mess of things with this woman,' Louis went on. 'And now we're not together any more.'

Penrose speared a prawn on the end of his fork. His eyes narrowed slightly. 'I'm sorry to hear it, but where do I come in?'

'We split up because she had a dream about an air disaster. The dream, in a way, came true.'

Penrose put down his fork. His eyes glinted with speculation. 'I take it you're a sceptic regarding such phenomena as extra-sensory perception, premonition, clairvoyance and so on,' he suggested to Louis.

'You could say that. I've always regarded people who claim to have special powers of the mind to be highly suspect,' Louis admitted. 'What was particularly worrying was that this dream of Diana's involved me. I had something of a starring role in it, even though she claims she had never met or seen me before. It led her to warn me very seriously against flying to New York for the wedding of my ex-wife. Oh, and that included a warning about my daughter going with me as well.'

'Pretty powerful stuff all round,' Penrose commented.

Louis took a sip of wine. 'Diana certainly found the dream powerful. In fact, it seemed to take over her life.'

'And at the same time, the two of you were falling in love?'

'Yes.'

'And did you fly to New York for the wedding?'

'No. My ex-wife decided to surprise me and our daughter by making a quick visit to London before the wedding. Her flight went down in the North Sea and she was killed.'

Penrose stroked a finger down the side of his wine glass. 'And both of you saw that as some kind of sequel to the premonition dream?'

'Correct.'

'And you instinctively put the blame on Diana for somehow being responsible for what happened?'

Louis closed his eyes. 'Yes.'

'And now — do you still blame her?'

'No. And I so much want to help her

through this, and for us to get back together.'

As Louis spoke, he knew Penrose was absorbing every word he uttered, weighing its meaning, forming theories.

'I was so cruel to her,' Louis went on. 'I drove her away.' He couldn't bring himself to mention Rupert, but he suspected Penrose might guess another man was involved.

Penrose sat in silent consideration for a few moments.

'So what is your question, Louis? In what way do you expect me to help you?'

'I want you to help me to understand about these psychic phenomena you spoke about. If I had more knowledge, then maybe I could understand all this better — and help Diana to come to terms with it.' He sighed. 'I'm really confused about what I think about all this dream stuff — it's like trying to grasp at a shadow.'

'Do you know what extra-sensory perception is?'

'Well, sort of. I think it means that people claim to have knowledge that doesn't come from the five senses — sight, hearing, touch, taste and smell.'

Penrose smiled. 'You're spot on. It basically means people can detect certain things by unknown means — such as dreams, or visions. I've spent a lot of time as a scientist trying to examine and describe these abilities in a way which would take the mystery out of them and hopefully neutralise the negative feelings around them from people like yourself.'

Louis grimaced.

Penrose frowned in thought, chewing on his bottom lip. 'Diana's dream strikes me as a form of ESP, perhaps the most curious and spine-chilling one. It's called precognition: knowing about things before they happen.'

Louis was about to follow up with a question but Penrose was already speaking. 'Tell me a bit about Diana — what sort of person is she?'

Louis considered. 'She is an intelligent,

warm woman, and a dedicated teacher. She's talented in speaking languages and playing the piano, and she's wonderful with children — ' He stopped abruptly, overwhelmed with a wave of longing for Diana.

'A capable and level-headed young woman?'

'Yes . . . But at the moment she seems to be driven by some curious force out of her control.' He looked up and caught Penrose's eyes resting on him with quizzical interest.

'So what you're saying is that if Diana could be helped to understand something about the way dreams can foretell the future, and how other people have experienced premonitions and dealt with them, then she might be able to view them in a more detached way?'

'Yes!'

'She would be in control of her power to have images of the future, rather than the other way round?'

'Exactly.'

'Let's look at the facts,' Penrose suggested. 'First of all, some basic biographical detail — Diana's age, background, parents, upbringing.'

As Louis answered Penrose listened intently, frowning in thought. 'Right,' he said eventually. 'So here we have an only child whose father died before she really got to know him. She was close to her mother, who you say is reported to have been highly superstitious . . . '

'Apparently. As a young child Diana was told not to walk under ladders, or look in cracked mirrors — and as for magpies it was all hell let loose if she or her mother spotted one on its own. You know the old saying — one for sorrow, two for joy . . . '

The professor nodded and sighed. 'And you mentioned that one single magpie had been sighted by her mother just before her sudden tragic death.'

Louis nodded.

'And perhaps for Diana herself, that tragic incident must have ensured that all of her mother's superstitions took on a new grim ring of truth.'

'Agreed.'

'And you say that Diana's mother was interested in clairvoyance and fortune-telling.'

'Quite hung up on it, apparently.'

'Mmm,' Penrose said, picking up his wine glass once more. 'My research has certainly indicated a strong link between certain early life experiences and the subsequent ability to predict future incidents. You see, I've inter-viewed over a hundred apparently sane people who claim to have powers of telepathy or prediction. But I didn't just talk to people and take their word for it; I also carried out tests in carefully regulated laboratory settings with observ-ers present. No trickery, no mirrors or white rabbits up sleeves.'

'How do you test powers of predic-tion?' Louis asked, fascinated now.

'The tests were very simple. They were based on human behaviour which was easily observable and could be simply recorded and then scored. For example I got people to predict the way a tossed coin would fall, or to correctly state the sequence of five cards laid down behind a screen out of their range of vision.'

'And then you compared the results with what would be expected to happen by the usual well known laws of chance?'

'Exactly.'

'And what did you find?'

'I regret to say that in the laboratory setting the results were disappointingly negative. I also looked at confirmed records of reported cases of premonition. There are one or two very dramatic and moving examples. A woman in Kent dreamed of the 1966 disaster in the mining town of Aberfan. It was a very clear dream, very clearly told. She saw coal hurtling down a Welsh mountainside. She saw a little boy at the bottom of the hill looking terrified. She saw rescue operations taking place. She had this dream seven days before the disaster. Two friends confirmed that she had related this dream to them, four days before the disaster.'

Louis felt a crawl of unease.

'And I was given another piece of evidence by a medical colleague. Her sister had died suddenly some years before. A year later, she had the sense that her dead sister was in the room. She looked exactly as my colleague remembered her, but she had a vivid red scratch on the side of her face. When my colleague told her parents about this, her mother became very distressed. Apparently she had put a rose in the sister's coffin and a thorn had scratched the dead girl's cheek. Allegedly no one else in the family had seen the body afterwards and no one knew of the infliction of the wound, which the mother had kept secret as she felt guilty. But of course we can't be absolutely sure on this point.'

Louis frowned, unsure what to make of all this.

Penrose was now in full flow. 'And also — according to her butler — Princess Diana wrote a message indicating that she would meet a violent death in some kind of crash. She wrote the message about a year before her tragic death in the tunnel in Paris.'

Louis nodded. He had heard of the Princess of Wales' prediction of her own end.

'So you see,' Penrose concluded, 'I'm not entirely sure what to make of my findings. And regrettably, clear and confirmed reports are rare. Reliable, unbiased witnesses are extremely thin on the ground. In a nutshell, the whole area is quite maddeningly problematic.'

'You spent a couple of years on painfully laborious research which turned out to be inconclusive?' Louis suggested with a rueful smile.

'That is the lot of scientists, but I had hoped for more definite results, and between you and me, I retired from the fray decidedly disappointed with the lack of hard-nosed evidence.'

'So did you actually unravel any mysteries of the mind?' Louis asked with a slight smile.

The professor's eyes twinkled. 'Maybe

not — but I wrote a cracking good book. And I'm just signing up to do a TV series.'

'Can't be bad,' Louis remarked. 'Have I wasted your time?'

'You could well ask if I've wasted yours,' Penrose answered. 'But I haven't finished yet. Along the way I learned a great deal about the human personality — the way in which the strength of evidence about those who claim telepathic or clairvoyant powers is influenced by their personal qualities.'

'And?'

'Basically the more ordinary, normal and sane-seeming is the person concerned, the stronger is the evidence for ESP, rather than some distortion of personality which makes that person want to attract attention to themselves by making extravagant claims, or to display signs of psychosis, in the form of delusions or hallucinations.'

'I see.' Louis recalled Diana's distress when they had first talked together about her dream.

You'll think I'm mad . . . a crazy woman with delusions.

'I'd rate Diana as pretty normal in terms of her personality,' Louis said. 'She's sensitive, but by no means neurotic.'

Penrose stretched in his seat, back arching, chest expanding, 'For what it's worth, Diana's disaster dream sounds like a potential example of premonition to me. The two flaws being that there was a possibility of having seen you in person before your first meeting, even though she didn't recall it, and if she had seen you, then her dream was more like a simple nightmare, and the resulting death of Poppy was simply a coincidence. More significantly, the dream did not predict Poppy's death. It suggested *your* death in an air disaster. Although I can see that Diana would have instantly made that connection at the time Poppy was killed.'

Louis nodded in acceptance. 'But if Diana has this ability for dreaming of disasters and it's causing her trouble, what can she do about it?'

Penrose took in a long breath and then let it out again. 'That's not an easy one. What I would advise is that she looks into her personal history — that could well be useful. If you get Diana to look into her past, her childhood years, somewhere there, she'll find a clue. Maybe something she has not recalled for many years.'

'The key to unlock the mysterious secret of her psyche,' Louis suggested in dry tones.

Penrose shot him a warning glance. 'Don't mock the paranormal,' he said. 'There's not a lot of evidence, as I've said, but there's enough to make us curious, and to resist dismissing the issue as the province of cranks.'

'I stand corrected,' Louis said. 'And I insist on paying the bill,' he added, taking out his wallet.

'You most certainly won't,' Penrose returned. 'You put your hand in your pocket and bought my book, and you've listened very carefully to all the stuff I've told you about a subject you find uncomfortable, so the least I can do is buy you lunch.'

Louis knew when not to insist. He was beginning to have quite a healthy regard for Professor Penrose.

'Do you think the dreams will stop coming for Diana?' he wondered aloud as they got up from the table.

'Yes, I believe they will. Very few people report more than one significant premonition dream. Not if they are genuine.'

Recalling Diana's words when they last spoke on the telephone, Louis took careful note of this information and filed it away in his memory for future reference.

'Has any of this been of help?' Penrose asked as they emerged into the busy street. He looked genuinely curious.

'Yes,' Louis said sincerely. 'Yes, it has.'

'Maybe you're not quite the sceptic you thought!'

'Perhaps not.'

They were now on the point of going their separate ways. Penrose turned around. 'Don't let Diana slip through your fingers,' he said abruptly. 'Not on account of a dream, however disturbing. She sounds like a woman worth fighting for.'

17

Diana named her puppy Elle; a simple, apt name — 'she' in French. Louis would have been entertained if he had known. Letting herself and Elle out of Percival's small east door, Diana braced herself against the raw hurt which always came when she allowed thoughts of Louis to come to the front of her mind, but it was impossible not to think of him and the hurting was almost constantly there.

Now, two days after her impulsive midnight phone call, she realised that the intense sensation of shared closeness that had sprung up instantly between her and Louis had almost seduced her into agreeing to leave Rupert.

And there lay danger.

She recalled Louis' pleading to let him come for her and felt a stab of grief. 'It's too late, my darling,' she cried out aloud.

'Too late and too dangerous.'

She had got up very early, wanting to get out of the house and avoid any danger of a further bedroom confrontation with Rupert. The puppy ran along beside her, scenting the morning breeze which was full of damp, earthy fragrances. Looking up, Diana saw the intricate skeletons of the trees, their leaves were almost gone. Looking back, she saw dark wavering tracks in the dew marking out the paths she and Elle had taken.

They walked along by the side of the fence enclosing the paddock. A grey mare and her foal stood side by side, gazing with steady concentration. When Elle spotted these strange, enormous creatures, she leapt back in amazement, her body rearing away from anticipated trouble.

Diana squatted down beside the quivering puppy and talked to her softly. Gradually the puppy's fear evaporated and suddenly she lost all interest in the horses and was springing off in search of new entertainments — darting squirrels and the odd strutting pheasant.

Her life is just beginning, thought Diana. *Everything is enchanting and wonderful.* The puppy's insatiable desire for new knowledge and sensation made Diana smile, and warmed her chilled heart for a brief moment.

She felt her life spiralling down into monotonous resignation as she became more convinced that some cruel force of destiny was working day and night to ensure she was denied the bliss of spending her life with the one man she loved.

The dreams were becoming tyrants; like stalking intruders they penetrated her sleeping mind, and filled her waking hours with anxiety and fear. She struggled to think of a way out of the bewildering maze of her subconscious mind, but who could she turn to? Only a few months before, she had considered herself a perfectly normal, rational person, someone who could cope with the problems life threw up.

The two premonition dreams had changed all that, but there was a new and sinister facet to the latest dream. It kept recurring — not every night, but with a random frequency that kept her in a state of suspense. She could never be sure when it might come, spiking her sleep with disquiet, demanding that she heed its insistent message. The dream crushed her spirit, not simply because of its drama, but because the message it contained told her that her hopes of happiness were all dashed.

Foolish and hysterical, she mused. *Is that what I have become?* Maybe she could get some shrink to unravel her emotions and get her back on track. Psychiatrists delved into people's past, didn't they, digging out all the ghostly skeletons from the cupboard and drawing their fangs?

Foolish and hysterical — the words kept repeating in her head. She stood quite still for a moment, concentrating. Elle, ahead of her, stopped too, observing her mistress with attentive and puzzled eyes. The words in Diana's head were spoken in a man's voice. The tone of voice was ironic, yet gentle and affectionate. She smiled in sudden recall: it was her Uncle William she could hear, her father's younger brother.

She remembered how he used to tease her mother, mocking her endless stream of superstitions, her incurable addiction to fortune-tellers and tarot readers, and yet he had never been unkind, never put her down.

The connection with Uncle William had dwindled over the years. After Diana and her mother moved south, they had only seen him at special family celebrations. She judged it must be four or five years since she had seen her Uncle William.

The puppy bounded up to her and she fondled its velvety ears. Her mind was active with new speculation, a tiny flicker of light glimmering at the end of a dark tunnel. It came from a spark of intuition that Uncle William might be the spring to activate some lever on her behalf — to transform the frail flicker of hope into a flame.

She wandered back down the length of the paddock, becoming more and more convinced of the need to go to Yorkshire in order to talk to Uncle William. He might be able to give her some clues to work on; some signposts from the past which would help her fight the demons of the present. Excitement surged within. New hope.

She guessed that she could get to Leeds on the train in less than three hours. She could have a long talk with Uncle William and still be back in time to have supper with Rupert and his parents. Rupert need never know a thing about it.

She let out a tiny moan of distress. How was it that she felt the need to employ such concealment and deception with the man she was going to marry? Why should she keep the Yorkshire trip a secret? She couldn't say — but she knew she was not going to tell him.

Doubts about her Yorkshire project began to set in, fear of what she might discover. She pushed them away. She had no commitments that day, it was school half term and Rupert had mentioned previously that he was going up to his London club to meet friends for lunch. She had nothing to lose by going.

By the time she arrived back at the house, she had made a definite decision. If she could contact Uncle William and he was happy about her plans, then she would hesitate no longer.

She rubbed Elle down with a towel in the back kitchen. *Who is going to look after you?* she thought, looking at the puppy with affection. Not Rupert, she decided. Quite apart from his plans for the day, he would consider that looking after Elle amounted to shutting her up somewhere and telling her to be good.

His parents were little better, fully engrossed in their various rituals for each day, and there was something about them which made her want to keep a slight distance and preserve her independence.

Rupert was standing in the hallway scrutinising the morning paper. Elle bounded up to him and deposited muddy paw marks on his trousers, for which she received a few sharp smacks and some extremely rude language. 'You'll have to teach this little bitch a few manners!' he commented cheerily to Diana, bending to kiss her lips.

Diana stiffened. Automatically she turned her face slightly so that his lips made contact with her cheek. 'I shall teach her everything necessary to make her socially acceptable. You don't have to worry on that score, Rupert,' she said with careful politeness.

'Angel! You're mad at me for tapping the dog's butt!' He threw his head back and guffawed. 'I didn't know you could look so thunderous.'

Diana forced herself to smile. She told herself for the hundredth time that Rupert was basically a good man and that he was harmless.

He regarded her with cheery, good-natured lust. 'Mmm, my angel, I could really fancy some serious love action when you're looking so fierce.' He gave her a smile of pure, sweet seduction, with his long lazy grin.

Diana stared back at him. She felt her features tighten.

He surveyed her through half-closed lids, his blue eyes gleaming with anticipation, his thick lock of custard-blonde hair falling enticingly over his forehead.

Ah yes, thought Diana, *there would be plenty of women who would be only too willing to fall into his arms.* She looked away from him, focusing every shred of her attention on her puppy. Elle looked up, her treacle-coloured eyes full of trust.

Marisa, thought Diana in a sudden rush of inspiration. Marisa would take care of Elle whilst she dashed up to Yorkshire. Marisa loved making dogs happy, and the eccentric Risk would be ecstatic. There would be fun and joy all round.

Moreover Marisa would be just the one to offer some good advice before she finally set off. And, last but not least, Marisa's house was next door to Louis'. Diana would not see him at all, but for a few moments she would be there in the vicinity of his house, looking out on the same street, the same trees and sky on which he looked out.

Diana breathed deeply. For the first time in weeks she felt as though she were driving her destiny instead of the other way round. Smiling up at Rupert, she linked her arm in his. 'I've decided to go up to Yorkshire,' she told him cheerfully. 'To see my Uncle William.'

'Splendid!' he exclaimed. 'Excellent! I just wish I could come with you, angel, but you know how it is . . . '

'Of course. You've a busy day planned in London. I'll be perfectly fine.' She touched his hand. 'And I'll be back this evening.'

18

Marisa and Risk returned from their early morning walk, a round trip of two miles through North London's residential streets and a nearby small park adorned with dusty shrubs and weary-looking roses.

It had been something of a trial, owing to Risk's rowdy confrontations with other terrible-terrier types with whom he liked to engage in a deeply fulfilling snap and snarl session before being dragged away by Marisa with the growls still choking in his throat. Then there were the cats, lurking in door-ways, winding him up mercilessly before nipping up gracefully into the security of a tree.

As Risk settled happily in his basket, Marisa made coffee, feeling she had truly earned it. She sat at the table, savouring the fragrant hot drink while pondering the clues of a half-finished crossword.

When Louis called a little later, it took a few seconds before she was able to pull herself from three down, the clue being 'lost horizons' which persisted in eluding her, and respond to the gentle knocking on the door. He came through into the kitchen, hollow-eyed and gaunt looking.

'Sit down,' she told him, fixing another coffee and offering him her cookie tin. 'Where's Sofia? Isn't it half term?'

'She's gone to stay with a friend. They're all going off to Brighton for a family holiday.'

'Nice.'

'Yes.' A long silence.

'Are you lined up for a photo shoot today?'

'The bike's in for a service. I thought I'd have a day at home, catching up with the paperwork.'

'Ah,' she said. Another long silence followed. It seemed to be a huge effort for him to speak. Marisa could see that his mood was dark and bleak.

'Louis,' she said with soft urgency, 'you look as pale as death, as if you haven't eaten or slept properly for weeks.'

He looked her in the eye, his dark eyes watchful and full of hurt. 'Diana's been in touch with me. Just this weekend.'

'I see . . . '

'She telephoned. It was well after midnight. She sounded so . . . so alone.'

Marisa got up and made a show of preparing more coffee. This was difficult for her. Diana had been in touch with her too; in fact, she would be arriving at the house with her puppy any time now.

Marisa had assured her that Louis would be out working. Well, wasn't he always? And if, for any reason, he was at home, then the bike would be parked outside indicating his presence. In which case, Diana would have to make her own decision about taking the risk of seeing him once more.

She glanced across at Louis, a lion in pain. What should she tell him? Should she try to manipulate the situation — persuade Louis of the benefit to be gained from a meeting with Diana? Or should she regard them as two wounded people for whom a meeting would be harmful at this point? Maybe she should go as far as trying to prevent it.

She hesitated, pulled between the two courses of action. Eventually she sat down, having reached the conclusion that there was nothing to be done except to simply allow events to take their course.

Louis was looking at the crossword. He pencilled something in, at the same time saying, 'I spoke to a guy yesterday who has just published a book on psychic experiences and premonition dreams. He's done some rigorous and scientific research on the subject.'

'Really! Where did you find him?'

'I spotted him doing a signing for his new book in a shop in Oxford Street. I bought the book, then hung around to talk to him. He gave me a lot of information and I've been up all night reading the book.'

'And?' Marisa prompted.

He shook his head and shrugged. 'I don't know. When I spoke with the author yesterday I felt buoyed up and full of new hope that I can somehow mend all the broken bridges with Diana.' His face was drawn and desolate.

'But?' Marisa asked.

'She's built a rampart around herself. She won't let me in. She doesn't answer her mobile, or my texts, and when I spoke to her for those few moments I could tell there was some new problem barring the way forward.' He put his head in his hands. 'She's with another guy now and she's going to marry him. It just doesn't bear thinking about . . . '

In the following moments of despairing contemplation, a knock came on the door and Risk exploded from his basket, a wiry bundle of raised hackles and frenzied barking.

'Excuse me,' Marisa told Louis, pursuing her dog down the hall and seizing him by the collar. Taking a deep breath she opened the door.

'Oh, my goodness!' gasped Marisa, hanging on for dear life as Risk struggled to get to Elle.

Diana was having similar problems, her puppy thrashing and bucking at the end of the lead like a frantic hooked trout.

'Come in!' Marisa said, grabbing Diana's hand and pulling her through the doorway. 'Everything will be fine in a minute. Just let Elle go. As soon as Risk has a chance to find out what gender she is, all hostilities will cease, I assure you.'

Diana was rosy with all the excitement and confusion. Her dark hair swung against the collar of her emerald-green coat and her eyes were alive with the pleasure of watching her puppy.

Watching her, Marisa wished she had been gifted with the talent for portrait painting.

A sudden heavenly silence fell as Risk's nose informed him that he was in the presence of delightful young female. His rumbling growls turned to grunts of pleasure. Diana began to move forward, her gaze following the two dogs.

She stopped dead and inhaled sharply when she saw him; a tall, still figure darkly outlined against the light from the far French window overlooking the garden. She saw the stunned wonder in his face — pure dazzling joy. A perfect replica of her own feelings.

Sliding past the dazed couple, Marisa shepherded the ecstatic dogs through the kitchen and into the garden. 'There are times,' she told Risk and Elle, settling herself on the wooden bench festooned with glistening golden leaves, 'when three is most definitely a crowd.'

★ ★ ★

Diana moved towards Louis, dreamlike and compelled. He opened his arms and enclosed her. His lips caressed her hair, her forehead, her cheeks. His fingers traced the path his lips had taken. 'The real you,' he breathed. 'Not just a voice, not just a picture in my head. Really you.'

Diana gazed at him. He had spoken words echoing exactly what she herself had been thinking. 'Your hair has grown,' she said. 'So silky and thick.' She reached up and stroked the shiny strands. 'It's a mane!' she laughed.

'I needed something to keep me warm,' he said meaningfully. He gathered her close to him again. 'Diana, Diana,' he murmured over and over again.

Diana sighed, hardly able to believe what she was seeing and hearing and speaking.

Moments passed, filled with pure sensation.

Slowly she pulled back from him. 'I have a train to catch,' she said with rueful appeal.

'What? Where are you going? My darling — you don't imagine I've any intention of letting you out of my sight, do you?'

Diana laid her hand flat against his chest. She could feel his heart leaping beneath her palm.

She began to explain to him about going to see her uncle in Yorkshire. Embarking on a journey into her past. It was important and she was full of hope. She looked up at Louis, no longer fearful, defying him to be angry.

There was concern and puzzlement for a time. She could see that he had been in terrible pain and that he was still uncertain and hurting. She was keenly aware, too, that she might have no choice but to hurt him further, and yet some strange vital hope for their future was still there, frail but glimmering.

When she finished speaking, he responded simply, 'Then I shall go with you.'

'Oh! Oh, Louis, I don't know . . . '

'I'm coming,' he told her. 'You can't stop me.'

Outside in the garden, in her thin shirt and jeans, Marisa chaperoned the cavorting dogs and shivered. The wind was sharp and raw, rattling the branches of bushes and whipping around chilled hands and arms. Marisa wrapped her arms around herself.

The autumn wind was truly predatory and bitter, yet somehow filled with promise. The crisp air, pungent with the scent of rotting leaves, smelled also of freshness and damp, of dark earth and smoke and petrol and rain. The complex scent of a living, breathing city.

Marisa breathed in deeply. She looked at the dogs; one old, one nearly new. They had rapidly established a ritual of play. They pranced together in a frenzy, then stopped dead, eyeing each other, teasing and testing, preparing for the next bout. Their hot breath curled up from their muzzles like white smoke.

Marisa smiled. She imagined the couple inside. Would they too be testing and teasing — preparing for the next bout?

'Life,' she murmured. 'But please God, don't let Louis and Diana take too long to come to some kind of decision.'

She thought she would prefer not to die of hypothermia — and then, suddenly, the answer to the crossword clue popped into her head.

Forgotten Dreams.

19

They spoke very little at the beginning of the journey. It was enough simply to be together, their fingers entwined. Diana felt Louis' gaze on her face. She could hear in her mind the questions that he was surely longing to ask. She tightened her fingers over his.

We are together, she thought. *Our hearts and minds are perfectly in tune.* We just live for these precious moments. The past has sunk back into memory, and as for the future . . .

The train was gathering speed now, carving its way up the spine of England. She leaned back in her seat and glanced once again at his face. Suddenly the shared moments of joy and breathless love in the spring came roaring back, unstoppable. And not just the exquisite tender moments she and Louis had shared, but the evenings with Sofia, the wonderful feeling of belonging in the beating heart of a family.

'Sofia?' she said to him softly. 'The schedules have changed now. I don't visit her school any more. Does she . . . ever talk about me?'

'No,' he said. 'But I think she hopes.'

She knew his answer had been formed carefully so as to manipulate her emotions and make her change her mind about coming back to him. She tore her gaze away from him and stared fixedly out of the window, vaguely registering huge fields and cows and a vast stretching sky.

'Are you sorry that fate seems to have brought us together again?' he asked quietly.

She tried to frame sentences, to explain to him the many different things she was feeling. It was impossible.

'If you'd seen the bike parked outside my house and known that I wasn't at a safe distance working, would you have turned round and gone away?' His eyes were cool and quizzical.

Diana was not entirely sure of the truthful answer to this question. What would she have done?

'I think I would have gone away,' she murmured.

'Avoided me?'

'Yes.' She unwound her fingers carefully from his. 'You know why, Louis.'

'I'm not sure I do.' He thrust his abandoned hand into his pocket, his face tight and closed.

'Because our lives have changed.' She hesitated. 'After Poppy's death, everything changed for us.'

'Yes. I was a crass, insensitive fool,' he said violently. People across the aisle turned and stared for a moment.

'No, you were in shock and grief, and you were very angry.' She glanced out of the window again. 'You were angry with fate, but you thought you were angry with me.'

'Yes, you're right.' He liked her clear-minded summing up, but he needed to build on it. 'We have no choice but to live with fate and go forward with the rest of our lives. We have to simply deal with what fate dishes out. But accepting fate doesn't mean we allow it to ruin the rest of our lives.'

'Things have moved far beyond that,' she said softly.

He pushed his hand through his hair in a gesture she knew so well. Every tiny gesture seemed delightful to her, reminding her of how deeply drawn to him she was.

No! I mustn't let him persuade me, she told herself in panic. *I mustn't let everything start up again between us and then have to go through the agony of parting from him again.*

'Yes, things have certainly moved on,' he retorted bitterly. 'For a start, you've promised to marry a man I know you don't love, a man who can't possibly have any idea of how to appreciate you.'

She flinched. 'That was brutal, Louis.'

'Why in heaven's name did you do it, Diana? I couldn't believe it when I found out. I still can't. Surely what we had together . . . '

'Stop it,' she whispered fiercely. 'You know perfectly well how much I loved you.'

'Why, then?'

'When you left me that night Poppy died, you looked as though you hated me — as though I were a stranger to you.'

A tiny nerve flickered at the side of his mouth.

'You looked as though you'd have preferred it if I had been the one to die, not Poppy.'

'Dear God! Now who's being brutal?'

'You thought because I had dreams and premonitions that a part of me was slightly crazy.' She stared at him, her eyes bright with challenge.

He said nothing.

'You thought it weakness at first. Female frailty, perhaps?'

He heard the strong accusation in her voice, her total rejection of the guilt she had been willing to carry on his behalf following that terrible night of Poppy's death.

'I admit it,' he said slowly. 'Your dreams and visions seemed to be a part of you that was secret and closed to me. I could never make myself understand it, so I rejected and despised all those things. I told myself they weren't part of you, the real you.'

She sighed. 'And when she died, you thought it was some kind of witchcraft. You thought I had worked some evil magic?'

The people across the aisle had their ears well pricked now. Diana was talking softly, but her tone was urgent and certain words chimed out — evil, witchcraft. Curious faces turned towards them once more.

Louis glared back at them with such ferocity that the would-be observers blushed with shame and returned to their newspapers. He took Diana's hand again. 'Yes, I admit all that and I beg to be forgiven.'

Ripples ran across her skin and she squeezed his fingers.

Louis' mind seethed with more

questions about Rupert and, even more urgently, what Diana had been trying to convey to him in that desperate phone call, which was clearly something highly significant.

After talking with Professor Penrose, he was pretty sure he knew what it might be.

'Let's just focus on today,' he said softly, exerting massive self-control.

'You'll like Uncle William,' she said after a brief pause.

'I won't intrude, Diana, if you'd prefer to see him on your own. There are plenty of things I can find to do.'

'Oh!' she exclaimed, remembering. 'Your artists and the plans for a gallery. Of course! Marisa told me.'

'Marisa seems to have been a good means of communication between us,' he remarked. 'I don't have any plans for art-empire building today, but I can always while away a few hours on the street with the Nikon. Real, hands-on work.'

'I want you to come with me,' she

said unexpectedly. 'There are things that I need to ask him that will be easier if you're there with me.'

'Truly?'

'Yes.'

They looked at each other. Louis leaned across and kissed her very firmly on the lips. As he straightened up she watched him with great tenderness. They sat together in silence once more, two people in perfect harmony.

As they pulled into the station and the train braked hard, bracing itself for the buffers, Diana touched his arm. 'When we were together before,' she murmured, 'I sometimes kept things secret from you. It was because I was afraid.'

'There's no need to be afraid. Not now, not ever. You know that, Diana.'

She gave a brief knowing smile. 'Perhaps. But whatever else happens — no more secrets.'

★   ★   ★

William Peach lived in a small flat over a bakery in one of the maze of tiny streets close to Leeds city centre.

Paying the taxi driver and looking up at the huddle of small red brick houses, Louis was surprised; he had imagined Diana's relatives would live in suburban affluence.

The entry to William's flat was at the top of a narrow flight of steps built against the outer wall of the side of the building. William was waiting for them in the open doorway at the top.

'Little Diana!' he exclaimed, kissing her cheek. He looked over her shoulder. 'Aha — who have we here? You didn't tell me you were bringing the lucky man along too.'

Diana turned, grimacing. 'Sorry,' she mouthed to Louis.

He smiled and walked forward to take William's hand. 'Louis Rogier,' he said. 'I'm very pleased to have been able to come and meet you.'

William led them through into a small sitting room. A large gas fire glowed on one wall, everything was neat and tidy and polished and a small round table was laid out with a dainty afternoon tea. There were tiny triangular sandwiches, freshly baked scones thick with butter, slices of fluffy sponge cake and a rich fruit cake.

Diana was instantly taken back to the Sunday afternoons of her childhood. Uncle William had lived in a little bungalow on the other side of town then. He and his wife Jean had run a very successful bakery and tea room.

Sunday had been their only day off, when they did 'their own private entertaining', as Jean had called it.

Diana recalled how close Jean and William had been. Jean had died a few years after Diana's father and for a while she had assumed, with a child's logic, that William and her mother would marry each other.

'Sit down, sit down,' William told Louis, who was standing at the window looking down into the street, assessing the possibility of some interesting shots.

William went into the kitchen and there were sounds of spoons and a teapot lid clinking.

Diana walked around the back of Louis' chair and ran her hand lightly over his hair. She sat down, still watching him and he raised his eyebrows and gave a slow half-wink.

William reappeared. 'Sugar and milk, Louis? Diana doesn't take sugar, if my memory serves me correctly.'

'It does indeed,' Louis smiled. 'She doesn't. And nor do I, thank you.'

'I like a man who gets straight to the point,' William said affably, pouring the tea.

Watching her uncle, Diana could see very little difference from when she had last seen him. He was one of those people who hadn't changed much at all since he came into middle age. He would be about sixty now, she thought, a small and wiry man with a mobile, leathery face, deeply grooved with laughter lines. His thick hair was a brilliant silver-white, but his eyebrows were still dark, making a startling contrast.

'What's she told you about me, then?' William asked Louis. 'Black sheep of the family, eh?'

'Not at all.'

'No, I was just having you on. I was never rascally enough for a black sheep. I'm a bit of a plodder, me. That's why I'm at the poor end of the family, you see, Louis. There are rich Peaches and poor Peaches.'

Diana and Louis laughed.

'But we've all got hearts of gold.' William guffawed, pleased with his little jest. He flourished a plate in front of Louis' nose. 'Come on then! Have a scone. I baked them myself.'

Obediently Louis took one and praised it while William poured strong tea for them all.

Diana felt herself relax. She had been wondering how her uncle would react to this sudden and impulsive wish to visit him. She had imagined awkward moments too, especially with Louis coming along.

She realised there had been no need for concern. William was clearly delighted to see her and would happily chat away for hours, plugging any awkward gaps in the conversation, had there been any. And Louis, for all his tense and critical alertness, was the kind of man who would get on with anyone, regardless of style or wealth, provided they were solid and genuine in spirit.

She tried to imagine Rupert in the same situation, wondering what his reactions would be — outwardly polite, followed by a humorous hatchet job in the car later?

'You know,' William mused, 'it's a funny thing when people start to think of getting married. They seem to have this need to go back to their roots and talk over old times, to resolve things. Is that what you were after, love?' he demanded of Diana.

'I suppose so, yes.' But it was more serious than just a little talk about old times, she conceded privately.

William leaned towards Louis, conspiratorial, man to man. 'She's a deep one, is Diana, you know. Not just a pretty face.'

Louis gave a small smile.

'Diana's like my brother, her dad. He was deep too, and a bit of law unto himself.' William reached for another slice of cake and offered the plate round. He frowned, reflecting. 'And determined as well. Once he got an idea in his head, there was no budging him. That's how he made a tidy fortune, most likely.'

'You look pretty determined yourself,' Louis remarked.

'No,' William said dismissively. 'I'm just a plain old grafter. Diana's dad had that extra go-for-it instinct.' He stood up, dabbing at the crumbs on his trousers with a rose-printed napkin. Crossing to the small bureau standing against the back wall, he picked up the box resting on its top.

'Look, I dug out the family snaps. You'll be interested in these, I bet.'

The box was shiny and gold, tied with a bronze ribbon. Diana recalled such boxes being exchanged in the family at Christmas. Once the chocolates were consumed, the boxes were saved to store snaps in, a process that seemed light years away from the digital age. William placed the lid on the table and started sorting through the photographs.

'Now then, let's see. Here's one of you when you were a baby, Diana.' He handed it over, and continued rooting through the box. 'And here's my Jean, your aunty, at Bridlington. She looks frozen, poor lass, as well she might; because it was brass-monkey weather and blowing a gale — and that was in June!'

Louis leaned across. 'May I?' He dug out a handful of photographs and leafed through them, observing intently.

William continued his commentary, unstoppable like a faulty tap. 'And here's your mum, Diana, all dressed up for a wedding. She was a real looker, you know — and always so well turned out.' He inspected the photograph more closely. 'I have to confess that I had a soft spot for your mum. Of course, we used to have our little set-tos now and then. I never could go along with all that mumbo-jumbo about fortune tellers and the like.'

'You teased her mercilessly,' Diana answered.

'Well, it's nothing I regret. She needed to be told; she was a real sucker for those clairvoyant charlatans and she'd pay over good money to anyone to have her fortune told — and then she'd swallow what they told her, hook, line and sinker.'

'Yes,' Diana agreed, looking regretful.

'That was all very well, until she started taking you along with her.' William glanced across to Diana. 'Do you remember?'

'Vaguely.'

'Your dad didn't like it. He thought it could be dangerous and there came a time when he put his foot down.'

Louis' eyes were now intense with speculation.

Confronted with her childhood photographs and her uncle's bluff comments, Diana found her eyes suddenly swimming with tears. 'I'm sorry,' she mumbled, discreetly wiping the wetness from her cheeks.

'Aye, love! I didn't mean to upset you. I should have thought before facing you with all this lot, and you just a little orphan when all's said and done.' He patted her knee. 'Never mind, you've still got your Uncle William.'

Louis reached for Diana's hand. 'Are you all right?'

She nodded. Louis stroked her arm, then got to his feet.

'I'm going to leave you two on your own. You might want to have some time to yourselves. Will you excuse me, William?'

'Most certainly, but there's not much exciting to see round here, not for a French man of style who lives in London.'

'You'd be surprised,' returned Louis.

He picked up his camera case. 'I never go anywhere without my Nikon.'

'He's a professional photographer,' Diana told her uncle.

'Well, if I'd known I was with someone in the big league, I'd have kept my little snaps in their box.' William pulled a wry face.

Louis paused to kiss Diana very gently. His eyes were tender. 'I'll be back soon,' he told her before he turned and closed the door softly behind him.

William looked at Diana, cocking his head on one side. 'You just hang on to that young man. He's a diamond — and he's not after your money!'

Diana simply stared at him uncomprehendingly.

'You just think on it, lass. You must have inherited a tidy pile from your mum and there's plenty of fellows would be panting to get their hands on it.'

Diana thought about it and then smiled. Her money had never been one of her problems, but she had never allowed a man to get very close before Louis, and to be fair to Rupert, she didn't think he was a fortune hunter. After all she supposed he and his family would consider her wealth to be a welcome bonus.

'The way he looks at you,' William said. 'That's real love.'

'Yes,' Diana said softly. She was quiet for a moment. 'Uncle William, what was it that made my father put his foot down?'

William cleared his throat. 'Your mum took you to see this clairvoyant in York. She was just an ordinary house-wife, seeing people in her living room, but she'd caused a bit of a stir and there were articles in the local papers about her miraculous powers and things she'd said.

'Well, love when your mum came back from seeing this woman she was in a terrible state — ranting and raving and carrying on. Completely hysterical, she was. Your dad couldn't do a thing with her. He rang us in the end and

Jean and I went round to see what we could do.'

Diana waited, tense like wire. 'And?'

'From what Jean could gather, this clairvoyant had told your mum something about you; she'd made some prediction.'

'Can you remember what Jean said?'

William shook his head. 'Never had any patience for that kind of thing so I was only half-listening, really and can't recall. Is it important for you, love?'

'It could be . . . '

He pressed his lips together, concentrating. 'It was something to do with you coming to a time in your life when there'd be some . . . negative force over you. I think that was it.'

'Oh, God,' Diana whispered.

'There was something about you bringing some grief on yourself, bringing on a lot of unhappiness.' William shook his head. 'It's wicked if you ask me, for perfect strangers to be feeding women like your mum that kind of dangerous rubbish.'

'Was that all?' Diana asked urgently. 'Was there something else? Please think, Uncle William!'

He hesitated, looking highly uncomfortable. 'I seem to remember there was a death along the way in all this, but then there always is with these fortune-tellers. They like to shock; it pulls in the punters.'

'Did Aunt Jean say anything to suggest my mother had been told that I might be the cause of a death?' Diana asked, with calm emphasis. 'Either directly or in some other kind of way?'

William visibly flinched. 'No!' he cried in protest. 'No, of course not!'

He's protecting me, Diana thought. *I've asked the one question no one in the family ever wanted me to ask, and the reason they didn't want to me to ask was because the answer was 'yes'.*

It was at that point that Louis came back. Diana knew that William had said all that he would ever say on the subject. She smiled in greeting at Louis, attempting to conceal her mood, which had turned dark and subdued.

'Any good pickings?' William asked.

'One or two. What I'd really like to do is to take some shots of you,' Louis told him.

'Get on with you! Here? Shall I comb my hair? Do you need any special lights?'

'No, nothing special needed; just you and a dark background and this little angle poise lamp I have in my bag.' Louis began to assemble his basic equipment.

William stood against the wall, bolt upright as though he had just escaped from an army parade ground.

'So,' Louis said conversationally, pointing his camera, 'were you always a baker, William?'

'Man and boy.'

'What training did you have?'

'Training? You must be joking! I started at a big bakery as the floor sweeper. We worked a ten-hour day, six days a week.'

'So, you worked your way up the

hard way then?' Louis was almost dancing as he spoke — falling lightly on one knee, springing up again, twisting his body from side to side to get an angled shot — and all the time he was talking, questioning, listening intently to his subject's answers and drawing him out further until the tension drained away from William's spine.

His flow of talk started again and he forgot about the visual impressions he was creating as he simply relaxed and became himself again — a man who liked to talk about life.

Diana had not seen Louis engaged in his professional work before, and now she began to understand the secret of his artistry, his ability to allow his subjects simply to be themselves. She looked on, transfixed.

As they left to catch the train back to London, William grasped her by the arm and whispered urgently in her ear. 'You just hang on to him, love. You won't find another of that calibre in a hurry.'

20

Sleet was falling outside as they walked into the station. Diana turned up the collar of her coat. Louis drew her against him, warming and protective.

He settled her in a window seat. Quite soon she fell asleep, exhausted by the events of the day and soothed by the motion of the train and Louis' nearness.

Louis sat beside her, looking unseeingly out of the window. His thoughts were entirely of Diana and the afternoon they had spent with her uncle, sharing a brief journey into her past. He had not yet confronted Diana with any of the pressing questions that repeated themselves in his mind, but he knew that he must do so at some point — and soon, for the journey would be over in less than three hours.

An image planted itself into his mind,

of Diana parting from him, walking away. There was a flare of sheer panic as he contemplated that bleak moment. They had been so close today. One minute he had persuaded himself that the chasm which had opened up between them in the spring was now firmly closed, the danger over. Then in the next minute he had felt a sense of helplessness about the way forward.

It struck him that he had been through this before, struggling in the dark, lonely pit of shattered relationships. It had been at the time when he had begun to understand that Poppy really meant it when she said she was leaving him.

He knew Diana had been in that dark pit, too and that it was he who had put her there. He pictured her, anguished and deserted in her house as he roared away on his bike on that dreadful night after their quarrel; Diana broken, wounded and alone with angry words echoing all around her; Diana dangerously vulnerable, ready to accept the solace of another man who had been biding his time . . .

The whole notion of this other man in Diana's life was hateful to him, an invasion of body and spirit. Little images flickered behind his eyes to taunt him: Rupert Pym touching Diana, possessing her. He gave a vicious little jerk of his head as if to clear out the pictures within.

The sharp movement woke Diana. 'What is it Louis?' she asked, immediately catching his mood.

He made a small noise like an animal in pain.

She took his hand, stroking it with soft fingertips.

'You're planning to leave me when we get into London, aren't you?' he asked.

Her fingers stilled. She looked away, avoiding his eyes. It was all the answer that was needed and he gave a low groan.

Diana sat in quiet contemplation. Her seeming calmness driving him mad.

'Explain!' he demanded. 'Tell me why you're going to do this terrible thing.

Make me understand.'

'I don't know if I can explain. I think we're looking at this situation through different eyes.'

'You call two people planning to tear up the roots of their happiness together a 'situation'?' he demanded, challenging.

'I didn't mean to sound heartless,' she said.

'Very well, I accept that. So, go ahead, Diana. Give me a good, sound reason — explain why you're going to leave me and go back to Rupert.'

Her face twisted with pain. That, at least, gave him a small particle of comfort.

'You told me there were going to be no more secrets for us two. So tell me the very worst.' He was relentless now, intent on making her tell him the truth. 'You've had another of your premonition dreams, haven't you?'

'Yes,' she whispered. She swallowed hard, then turned her head towards the window and began to speak, resting her gaze on her own pale reflection, though she hardly noticed it; what she was seeing was a memory of the pictures inside her head.

'For a few weeks now I've been having this same dream, over and over.' Her eyes flickered towards his, cautious and fearful.

He nodded and gave a small smile of encouragement. This time he would really listen, try to tune in with her feelings.

'I have this sensation of being in water. I'm in some great lake, I'm swimming and I feel so free. It's a wonderful feeling, like flying on one's own wings. There's a man with me, swimming ahead. He looks around to make sure that I'm following, that I'm safe.'

'And who is this man?' Louis asked.

'I can't see his face. He's wearing a diver's mask, just as I am. All I know about him is that I want to follow him wherever he goes.' She paused. 'So it must be you.'

Louis sighed.

'We're in a lake where there used to be a village. As we swim down we can see houses, and a road. There's a drowned church with a tall, pointed spire. The man is swimming down to the ruins. He has a lamp on his mask and its beam draws me on.

'This man is a very strong swimmer and I start to fall behind.' Here she stopped, uncertain how to continue. She wanted to paint the clearest picture for him, but it was at this point the dream always became cloudy.

'Go on,' Louis urged softly.

'My legs begin to feel heavy and lifeless. The more effort I make the more deadened they feel, quite immovable. I want to go towards the light, but I have no power in me.'

She closed her eyes. 'I see a dark shadow pass above. It's the hull of a great ship and its rudder is churning the water and black smoke pours out of a pipe in its side. I feel paralysed with fear as a man's body falls from the ship.

He's wrapped in a sack, struggling and shouting, but the sack is tied so tightly he can't escape. There's no one to help him, except me. He shouts at me in terror and panic, 'Diana!' he calls. Somehow I make a great effort and I manage to swim up to him and I start to untie the bag so as to free him to swim up to the surface. The man inside is Rupert . . . '

She finished her story and bowed her head. 'Do you understand?' His eyes blazed as she looked up. 'Please, Louis, don't you see the meaning of this dream?'

'I think I know the meaning that you see in it,' he said slowly.

'Then tell me,' she said, barely audible.

'You see two men in your dream. You see me and Rupert. You're drawn to me, but something holds you back and that something is Rupert. You see that he needs you, that he's in danger and only you can be his saviour.'

She let out a great sigh. 'Yes.'

'It won't do, Diana. It's not a reason to destroy our chances of happiness. It's simply a dream.'

'No. My previous dreams were prophecies of some sort, and they came true.'

'No! They did not come true in the literal sense. Neither Sofia nor I were killed as you had feared.'

'No, but Poppy was and she was your ex-wife; you were once a couple, united in body and spirit. That's what marriage is supposed to be about.'

Louis made a swift, furious, negative gesture with his hands.

'Listen to me, Louis.' She grasped his wrist fiercely. 'You will listen to me.'

'Very well.' His voice was icy.

'I understand now that my premonitions are not literal in terms of precise details, but they're warnings sketched out roughly in my mind in ways I can interpret.'

He shook his head. 'No, Diana; these are utterly irrational conclusions to come to.'

'The foolish imaginings of a hysterical woman?' she cut in. 'Perhaps you would like to believe I'm like my mother, or at least that I share a part of her personality?'

He closed his eyes in denial as he struggled to keep his temper. 'I'm sorry. Go on.'

'I told you my dream of the air crash in detail and I told it to you weeks before it happened, then I warned you again just before the doomed flight — and my prophecy of disaster came true.' Tears of frustration glittered on her eyelashes. Why would he not see? Why would he not accept?

Again he shook his head.

'For heaven's sake, Louis, don't you see? Poppy — your wife, Sofia's mother — was killed in a terrible air disaster. She was killed just at the time I had dreamed there would be exactly that kind of crash. What more proof do you need?'

'Your dream was prophetic, I do accept that. In a general sense, but — '

'You insist on denying the truth before

your eyes. You're stubborn and obstinate because you like to believe you're a realist.' She felt herself grow hot with the effort of trying to convince him.

He drew in a breath and steeled himself. 'Diana, yesterday I spoke to a professor of psychology who has made a special study of premonition dreams, of people who seem to be able to know and predict things in their mind which other people can't.'

She stared at him, stiffening.

'He gave me a lot of information and I've bought his book, and read quite a lot of it . . . '

'Go on . . . '

'In a nutshell, he didn't think your dream fitted with some other reported precognition dreams.'

'Very well, then,' she cut in. 'If you don't believe in the power of my dream, Louis, then tell me this — why did you blame me for what happened?'

He turned away from her.

'If my dream was nothing more than a mere flight of fancy, then why did it lead to our splitting up?'

He was silent.

'You did have some belief, didn't you? You weren't quite the sceptic you make out to be?'

'Perhaps not. Although I don't pretend to understand any of these things you describe.'

She leaned her head against the seat, drained and exhausted. At least he had stopped fighting her at last.

He said, 'Are you saying to me that because of this latest dream you feel compelled to return to Rupert?'

'Yes.' Her eyes were dull and weary.

'That if you don't, then he might be in some sort of danger; some terrible disaster might befall him?'

'Yes, that is exactly it.'

'My God!' It was a cry of despair.

'I haven't had this dream just once, Louis. It keeps coming, a recurring dream . . . a warning.'

'What can I do?' he demanded. 'When you say things like that, I'm powerless.'

She shook her head in a gesture of

resignation he found utterly terrifying.

'There must be some way I can make you change your way of looking at things. Please, Diana.'

'How can I choose my own happiness when it involves taking the risk of exposing someone else to danger? How could I live with it if something dreadful happened to Rupert?'

'This is madness,' he warned her. 'I'd bet on it that Rupert is virtually indestructible.'

'He's a vulnerable human being, like the rest of us.'

Louis was so angry and helpless that he could hardly breathe. 'I simply can't believe you're going back to Rupert,' he told her. 'How can you do that, after this precious day we've had together?'

She would not look at him.

'What do you see in Rupert, for heaven's sake?'

'He's offered me stability and permanence. He was there when you pushed me away.'

'Okay, you had a moment's weakness.

You can't let your whole life hang on that.'

'I was destroyed, that night you left. You wrote me a letter that made my heart feel as though a stake had been driven through it.'

Louis felt himself freeze inside. There was a growing realisation that he would have to accept Diana's intentions. There was nothing he could do to change them.

He got up and went to the wash cubicle. Staring at his face in the glass above the basin he saw a man who was haggard, drawn and desolate. He could see the hope draining from him even as he looked.

He returned to Diana. She smiled at him with love and compassion, like a mother comforting a child who has suffered some terrible disappointment.

He sat down heavily, feeling cold and hard and cruel; in the mood for some straight talking. 'Have you made love with Rupert?' he demanded.

She said nothing. A flush crept into her face.

'I'm taking that as a yes,' he said.

She turned her head very slowly. 'Oh, Louis,' she said with deep reproach.

Louis felt a churn of nausea; gripped with raw jealousy, he could not see her response as anything but an affirmative to his question. Jealousy fired him, then burned him, a tormenting flame running back into his past and flaring into the future.

He covered his face with his hands. 'I don't think I can bear this,' he said bitterly.

Diana touched his arm. 'You never let me answer. You simply made assumptions.'

He looked up.

'I haven't made love with Rupert.' It was a whisper.

'Oh, Diana.' Gladness washed over him, followed by shame. 'I'm so sorry. Please forgive me. I'd no right . . . '

She laid her hand on his cheek.

'But he kisses you, he touches you,' Louis murmured.

'We are engaged,' she said in horrible distress.

'Sweet heaven, and soon you'll be married, then you will have to make love with him. Have you any idea how that makes me feel?'

She was unable to speak, her throat choked with grief.

'So what is going to happen when we get to London?'

She looked him straight in the eye and said nothing.

'I see. I have to watch you walk away and I go back to my empty house. Is that it?'

'Yes.' She bowed her head under his weariness and anger. She couldn't bring herself to tell him that Rupert had sent her a text, asking her to meet him at his currently favourite restaurant in Spitalfields.

Louis considered the nature of love. He thought of Poppy, he thought of Sofia, he thought of his feelings for the woman beside him, he thought of the words of Shakespeare: *Let me not to the marriage of true minds admit impediment.*

He pulled Diana into his arms, stroked

her hair and her face. 'Whatever else, I shall never stop loving you, darling. Even you can't make me do that.'

At the station he helped her into a taxi. Its paintwork gleamed oily black beneath the bright lights on the concourse, the reflections on the roof stretching and contracting as it moved away and merged into the flow of traffic.

Louis turned and walked towards the entrance to the Underground. He had made his final decision and he would not cease to hope.

21

Diana sat in the taxi, cold and numb. In London's central streets, in the clutch of the beginning of winter, all was light and warmth and gaiety. The Christmas decorations were already in place and the black darkness was spiked with coloured lights. She looked up and saw a giant iridescent clown's face, grinning at her through mocking blue lips.

Couples strolled together through the chilly streets, arms linked and pausing by the gleaming window displays when something caught their eye.

Diana imagined them discussing presents they would be buying for family and friends — for each other.

She opened her bag and felt around for the velvet box containing the ring Rupert had given her. She slipped it on, remembering how she had surreptitiously slipped it off that morning before she and Louis boarded the train. She knew Rupert had a keen eye for that sort of detail and would notice immediately if the ring he had given her was not in evidence.

He was waiting at the restaurant, lingering over a gin and tonic because Diana was very late. He stood up, looking annoyed rather than worried, but then worry often has that effect on people, she told herself.

'Angel!' He bent to kiss her. 'I've been hanging around for ages waiting for you. I began to think I was being stood up.' He laughed. Being stood up was just about unthinkable for him.

'I'm so sorry, Rupert. I had to get a later train than I'd planned.' The lie grated with her. Talking smoothly of 'I' when it should have been 'we'.

'You could have texted me from the train,' he said. 'It doesn't do much for a guy's ego to be sitting around like a bit of a lemon when a cosy table for two's been ordered.'

He was leaning back in his chair,

smiling at her lazily. His tone was fond and indulgent but Diana did not miss the hint of warning running underneath. He would not be at all pleased if she did this to him again.

'You're quite right,' she said. 'I should have let you know. I really am sorry.' Well, at least that was part of the truth. It would hardly do to tell him she had been on such an emotional roller coaster she had forgotten about Rupert, except when he figured as the veritable eye of the storm in her and Louis' confrontation.

She accepted a glass of chilled dry wine offered by the waiter and picked up the menu.

'I've already ordered,' Rupert informed her crisply. 'I'm simply famished.'

'Right.'

'I've asked for melon for you, angel, and the grilled sole to follow. Okay?'

'Yes, of course.'

Rupert tossed back the dregs of his gin, looked around and clicked his fingers. A waiter hurried up to pour out the claret.

Rupert took a long gulp.

Diana felt sweat prickle down her spine. The nasty sense of shabby deception was tightening its grip.

To come in such a short time from the arms, mind and heart of one man to the company of another — the man she had promised to marry — made her wince with shame.

She felt as though she were a traitor to both of them.

She picked up her glass of wine and a sudden wave of aching longing for Louis gripped her with the sharpness of a spasm of physical pain. She took some long breaths, steadied herself and sipped at the wine.

'You look a bit glum, angel,' Rupert remarked. 'Did the day turn out a bit hard going — not quite what you'd expected?'

She stared fixedly at her glass. 'You could say that,' she agreed. She found herself horribly torn and confused. She felt she could not abandon Rupert, that to do so would bring him terrible bad luck, even danger.

But at that moment she suddenly knew she could never marry him. Never. She loved Louis. Only Louis.

'I suppose so,' she said carefully.

She felt Rupert's eyes on her, watching, assessing. She swallowed hard.

'One of my chums from the bank has invited us to a drinks party tomorrow,' he told her. 'It should be fun and I'd like to show you off. What do you think, angel?'

She looked across at him, her face wistful and troubled.

I have to tell him, an inner voice said. *I have to!*

'Come on, eat up,' he told her. 'You need to keep up your strength for later on,' he added meaningfully.

This time she did not look up.

Do it now! her inner voice insisted.

'I've been doing a bit of talking with the parents,' Rupert suddenly announced.

She looked up in surprise. 'Oh?'

'Nothing to worry about, angel. Just boring money talk, but there's a general feeling that you and I need to take a little advice sooner rather than later.'

'Do you mean financial advice?' She laid down her fork.

'Yes. Before we marry. Sort things out a bit. Protection for both of us — after all, we're neither of us paupers.'

'You mean,' she said, 'that in case we should ever split up, then we should have it in black and white who gets what? A prenuptial agreement?' She could not believe it.

'It's simply good sense,' Rupert remarked, as if keen to sound low-key. 'Come on, angel, money's my profession. You can't expect me to close my eyes to all the implications involved when a marriage is in the offing.'

'No, you're right.'

'Good. So you'll be happy to come with me to see this guy my father recommends?'

'When do you plan to go?' Her tone was sharp.

'Oh, in a week or so — no rush.' He raised an arm to summon the waiter to bring the bill. 'Come on, sweetheart,' he chivvied affectionately. 'Smile! We'll be married soon enough.'

By now her heart was thumping so hard she felt that he would be able to hear it as she dully followed him from the restaurant to the street outside.

As they stepped from the enclosed warmth of the restaurant, making for Rupert's car, the freezing night air hit him like a slap. He staggered slightly, almost losing his balance. For a moment Diana thought he would fall into the road. A large passing car swerved sharply, anticipating trouble.

'Oh, my goodness!' she whispered, grasping his arm and staring up into his face, her own face tight with anxiety. 'Are you all right, Rupert?'

Rupert brushed her worries aside. 'Absolutely fine, angel. Only half of the nine lives gone — if that. Sweet of you to be so concerned,' he said.

Diana let him help her into his car and then sat rigid as he drove back to his flat. The incident with the near miss had seemed to confirm her worries about Rupert's safety. She tried to think things through, but her thoughts were flying all over the place, as impossible to capture as the wind.

In the hallway of the flat he took her coat and laid it over a chair, then poured himself a whisky. 'Drink, angel?'

She shook her head.

In her head, a mental videofilm was playing the image of Rupert about to go down in front of the wheels of a Range Rover, but her inner voice was speaking up again.

It was a simple accident. It was not your fault and your dreams are just dreams, nothing more. Louis is right. Rupert is fine and you're not going to marry him . . .

No way! Her own mind seemed to be determined to conduct and inner argument.

Rupert sat down. 'Come here, my sweet. You look bushed. Come and let Rupert take the strain.'

He opened his arms to her. The look

of desire on his face was mingled with a touch of triumph as if she had already given herself to him.

She looked at him, her heart jerking with feeling. Every nerve in her body was shouting *No!*

Suddenly a violent spasm seized her stomach. She rushed into the bathroom and was sick. Gasping with shock, she ran cold water into the washbasin and splashed it onto her face.

She stared at herself in the glass, seeing a white-faced woman with terrified, dark staring eyes looking back. A woman who had teetered on the edge of the cliff, staring into the abyss.

I have to take charge, she told herself. *I have to take charge of my dreams, of myself, of my own life and of my loyalty and love for Louis and for dear Sofia.*

My dreams are still a mystery to me, but what I learned from Uncle William and what Louis has told me has begun to make them fall into place, and to understand the shadow I was placed under as a child and how it has affected my life.

But bowing to the power of the dreams is a betrayal of myself. My unconscious might speak to me in seductive terms, but it is my conscious self that must make decisions about my life and the people I truly love.

She put out her hand and touched her reflection in the glass. *It is really much more simple than I thought,* she whispered to her image. *But I have to be very strong.*

She went to rejoin Rupert, who was sitting staring into his whisky and looking rather glum.

'I'm going to go back to my own home, Rupert,' she said quietly. 'And I'm breaking off our engagement.'

She took off her ring and slipped it into his hand. He stared at her, his brows drawn together in astonishment.

She sat down opposite him, and very quietly and honestly she began to speak. She told him she could not marry him because, although she was fond of him and always would be, he was not her true love. She explained that she had unwittingly used him to comfort herself at a time when she had been undergoing great turbulence and been in great need.

'I have behaved very badly towards you Rupert, and I'm deeply sorry,' she said with genuine regret.

As she spoke, she saw his expression change from one of concern, to one of disbelief. In his cheeks a rusty stain appeared. He got up, turned sharply away from her and went to stare out of the window. He thrust his hands into his pockets, jingling the coins there.

'Well, I say, this is a bit of a blow,' he said eventually. 'Are you going back to him? Your French guy?'

'Yes.'

Rupert gave a sharp, braying laugh as he swung round. The flush in his face had gone; he was himself again.

'Things haven't been exactly brilliant between us recently, have they?' he said to her. 'I'm not a complete fool; I know the writing's on the wall when the girl you're going to marry has to run to the bathroom to throw up when you lay a finger on her.'

She would not be drawn on this point. It was true, so what was there to be said?

'Can you forgive me, Rupert?' she said softly.

Rupert reached out and picked up the ring he had given her, turning the gold hoop through his fingers so that needles of light flashed from the stone.

Relief was flooding through him in great waves, enlivening him, astonishing him. Normally he hated to be the one given the push and moreover, he had fancied that Diana was the girl for him, but now, watching her beautiful, intense face, her big luminous eyes searching and penetrating his, he felt as though he had been sprung from a velvet-lined trap.

Vaguely he thought of a future where he would bring a handsome county set girl to Percival as his bride. She would fit in perfectly, be a lioness in bed, have sturdy babies and turn a blind eye to his occasional wolf-like prowling.

'Rupert,' she prompted. 'Say something, please.'

'You've astonished me, angel.' He faced her square on, and she could see a rakish gleam in his eye. She saw that, following his initital dismay, he was becoming rather interested in the notion of a return of his old bachelor freedom. She slumped against the back of the chair. *Oh, thank you, God.*

'No hard feelings?' he asked.

'Of course not.'

'Then I think you should go now,' he told her softly.

★   ★   ★

Louis paced the ground floor of his house. He could not bear to contemplate the torture of going to bed and lying awake seeing pictures of Diana as she had been on their day together, moving through a whole rainbow of moods, from shining gold to indigo as

303

she sat in the little room in Yorkshire being reunited with her past.

And now — Diana with Rupert.

The idea of it made him wince. When he pictured her in Rupert's embrace, the pain was like an electric shock.

He reminded himself that she had told him that he, Louis, was the only man who had touched her soul — that was something he must hold on to in order to survive the revived agony of parting with her and standing back while she walked into the arms of another man.

But he wondered whether Diana understood that for him, the thought of his dearest love being bodily caressed by someone else was indescribably painful.

He told himself she was not his to possess — and yet he had always despised men who thought of women in that way, as though were no more than enviable trophies — but with Diana, it had simply been a feeling that she *was* his, in just the same way that he was hers.

That any other man should possess

her, or any other woman claim him, was simply unthinkable — but now the unthinkable had become reality.

He decided to stop fighting against the pictures of Diana and Rupert together; he would let them come and do their worst. If you ran things over in your mind for long enough, then they lost some of their power, didn't they?

He went though to the kitchen and examined the contents of the fridge. He would do something practical; make preparations for Sofia's return from her brief holiday.

He picked up a knife, sliced an onion, peeled a clove of garlic, then he got out tomatoes and looked through his pots of herbs.

Later, at the sink, he carefully washed the kitchen knife and wiped down the chopping board.

Focus on the here and now, he told himself. *Take notice of the shape of this knife, the shine of the blade, the dull black of its handle.*

He waited for himself to grow calmer.

22

On the day following her break from Rupert, Diana spent the morning in quiet contemplation. She made herself hot chocolate and sat down to drink it at the table in her kitchen where she and Louis had shared precious moments.

She thought again of what her uncle had said the day before, and how the words of a fortune-teller in a house in a seaside town had been taken to heart as some kind of prophecy. A prophecy of doom.

Somehow, her mother had become convinced of some future unseen force that would brood over her innocent child. It seemed to Diana now that the story was reminiscent of the tale of Sleeping Beauty and the threats of the wicked fairy concerning the needle that would prick her finger.

Over time, her mother's anxieties had driven her to wrap her daughter in a cloak of protectiveness — a mantle of illusions and half-truths, of fantasies and dreams and irrational fears. Her mother had unknowingly taught to her see danger everywhere, and because she was her mother, the power of her influence had been awesome . . .

Diana looked up, surprised to find that the room was growing dark. She was chilled and stiff, her limbs and spine aching.

She got up and crossed to the window, realising that some hours had passed during her waking reverie. The setting sun was now a huge incandescent glow, about to be swallowed up into the dark horizon. In time a shaft of silver moonlight came through the window, laying itself across the dark shape of her sofa like a great silver sword.

Diana stared into the darkness, pulling at the threads of her recent thoughts, trying to draw them together into a knot of conclusion. *I have gone some way down the road which was marked out by my mother's footsteps,* she told herself.

My mother called and I followed. When I started out I was a child, and then a young woman struggling to find a path of my own. But now, at last, I've found the path I want and I must take it. I must go where the light beckons.

Suddenly the way ahead was clear.

Without any further delay, with no trace of fear, only a blissful anticipation, she took out her phone and dialled Louis' number.

★   ★   ★

Sofia had only just got back from her holiday in Brighton when her friend invited her for a sleepover and she was packing her little red case in preparation. She put in her toothbrush and toothpaste, her brush and comb and her nightdress.

She paused to think.

Louis came silently to stand in the doorway. 'Can I help?'

'Clean socks, vest, pants, change of shoes,' recited Sofia. 'That's what you always say, Daddy. And I've done my tooth things already.' She set about gathering the other articles she had mentioned.

'What time shall I collect you on Sunday?' he enquired.

'Melanie said four o'clock. And her mummy said you have to stay for a cup of tea and some cake.'

'Very well, I'll be there.' Louis smiled at her tenderly, feeling a surge of love and protectiveness. 'Melanie seems to be a good friend,' he commented.

Sofia looked at him. 'Yes.'

Louis hoped that her quick, instinctive child's understanding would fail to penetrate to the medley of emotions currently swamping him. Perhaps the only positive feeling was his pleasure at Sofia becoming a regular visitor to the home of a proper family — two parents, a brother and sister. Louis had often wondered whether Sofia felt lonely and cut off, with only a sad, troubled father for company at her own home.

'You're a very well-organised girl,' he observed, watching her lay her clothes neatly in the case.

'I'm very old in my head,' Sofia told him.

'What a strange thing to say.' He smiled. 'But yes, I think you're right.'

'It was Diana who said so.' Sofia's hands were still for a moment. She did not look up. Then she continued packing.

'I see. Well, then, Diana was right.'

Sofia turned. 'You said Diana's name — out loud.'

Louis felt a jolt. 'Yes, so I did.'

Sofia sat on the bed. She bowed her head and rubbed her hands over her knees. 'Daddy?' She hesitated. 'Can Diana come at Christmas?'

Louis' heart gave a buck — he hadn't expected this. He sat down beside Sofia. 'My darling, I'm not sure.'

'I want her to come, and you'd like her to come, wouldn't you, Daddy?' she burst out with feeling.

He could not speak and Sofia put her arms around him — not seeking comfort, rather offering it.

He felt a tightening in his throat. 'Oh, chérie,' he murmured.

'Will you ask and see what she says?'

He sighed.

They heard the sound of a horn outside and went down the stairs together, Louis carrying Sofia's bag. She turned back to look at him, the question still in her eyes.

It was a question Louis had already answered himself some hours previously following a restless, sleepless night.

★   ★   ★

Diana heard the tone buzzing rhythmically in her ear. She stood, the phone pressed against her face, just letting it go on, sure in her conviction that a connection would be made.

Voice mail eventually cut in and she laid the phone down. She imagined him, out on the road somewhere, or on his bike, or in the Underground. He was making his way home and had his phone switched off, but soon he would be home and contactable.

She pressed the call button again. Through the regular burrs of Louis' phone, she heard the ring of her own doorbell.

'Louis!' she called out instinctively.

She ran to the door, almost falling over the puppy in her haste to get there. She saw the tall black-clad figure through the glass and her heart leapt with joy. Gathering Elle into her arms lest she dash into the road, she greeted him, pulling him inside with her free hand, reaching up to give him a kiss.

'Oh, my poor darling!' he exclaimed, seeing her ruffled hair and her white face.

'No, I'm not poor and I'm not sick any more.'

He held her away from him. 'Something has happened, something quite new. Tell me. Whatever it is, you know you can trust me now.'

She laid the palms of her hands flat against his chest. 'I've discovered for the first time who I really am — and more importantly, who I want to become.'

Louis felt a prickle of sensation run across his scalp.

'And it's because of you, Louis,' she added. The words were said with quiet determination and simplicity.

His eyes moved over her face. 'You have me to thank? I felt that I was the one who had almost killed you.'

She shook her head. 'Your being there with me when I went to see my uncle — it was your presence and your thoughts all around me that made it possible for me to understand things about my past that have always been hidden and mysterious before — and it was knowing you would always be there for me, loving me, which made it possible for me to see the way ahead in the future.'

'Thank God,' he whispered. He drew her to him and kissed her until they were both dazed.

When at last they drew back a little, staring into each other's eyes, he asked, 'The dreams, are they still coming?'

He held his breath. Did this mean she was going to come to him for ever, that Rupert would become a figure of her past — or simply that she had learned to be at peace with herself whatever new obstacles were to be endured?

'I was becoming a slave to the images of my sleeping mind,' she said. 'A prisoner of my dreams.'

'And now?'

'Now it's time for me to believe in my waking mind and the reality of my eyes and ears.' She reached out and touched him with her fingertips; his eyelids, the hard straight line of his nose, the warmth of his neck, the firm broad shoulder bones.

'This is real,' she breathed, pulling his head down to hers.

For long, wonderful moments they moved together, locked in a slow dance of joy, love and deep commitment.

23

In Louis' kitchen the enticing fragrance of roasting goose and lemon stuffing stole from the kitchen and curled itself around the hallway and the ground floor.

From either side of the oven, a small wiry dog and an ever-growing red setter puppy occupied themselves in soaking up the bliss-making smells. From time to time one of them would shift a paw, or twitch an ear, whereupon the other would open an eye with renewed hope.

Sofia sat cross-legged close by, reading a story about a naughty terrier called Hairy Harry and from time to time breaking off to look lovingly at the two dogs — and then to take yet another sidelong peek at the Christmas tree, which she could just see down the hallway.

Meanwhile Diana and Louis were

putting up the last of the Christmas cards and then making a start on setting the table for the Christmas Day lunch. In the sitting room the flames from crackling logs threw flickering shadows on the wall.

Everything was now in place, ready for the arrival of Marisa and Professor Penrose.

Louis had contacted the professor to tell him how much he had benefited from talking to him and reading his book. The professor had been delighted to hear his news, and when it turned out that Professor Penrose was planning on spending Christmas Day alone, Louis had immediately invited him to join the newly formed Rogier family for lunch.

Diana stood with Sofia and the instantly watchful dogs as Louis took the bird from the oven, basted it, poured off the excess fat from the tin and slotted the potatoes in to roast.

'A man who takes brilliant photographs and presides over an up and coming art gallery shouldn't be able to cook like a wizard as well,' she commented in teasing appreciation. Happiness flowed between them, the simple joy of being together.

Louis surveyed the trails of holly and the glinting cutlery and glasses on the table and had a sudden memory of the year before. 'Christmas last year was just a lonely man keeping company with his sad little girl,' he said softly. 'But this year we're going have a party!'

Diana smiled to herself as she set out shiny crackers on each side plate. She thought of the presents waiting under the tree in the hall where the floor was already showered with fallen needles. She felt an almost childlike thrill of expectancy at the magical prospect of the expressions on Sofia's face when she opened her presents. For Diana, too, recent Christmas Days had been wistful affairs.

Marisa and Professor Penrose both arrived at the door promptly at one o'clock.

'Is my wicked dog behaving himself?' Marisa asked Sofia, handing over some extra last-minute presents to be placed underneath the tree.

'Yes, he's been perfect. In fact, he's been so lovely, we might want to borrow him again!' Sofia gave Risk an affectionate hug.

'You can borrow him any time,' Marisa said. 'I think he rather likes it round at your place — something to do with having a furry girlfriend to keep him company!'

Sofia stroked Elle's long, silky ears. 'I think Elle really likes me,' she said. 'Diana lets me give her her food, and last night Elle was allowed to sleep on my bed.'

'This is just like old times, when I was young,' Professor Penrose exclaimed, beaming. 'A real family Christmas.' He raised a glass to the assembled company, his eyes twinkling with seasonal goodwill.

★ ★ ★

Later, when they were all full of goose and pudding, they set out for a walk in the park. The air had turned cold and a sparkle of frost lay on the pavements like sieved icing sugar.

Louis and Diana walked with their arms around each other. Sofia, who had been hanging on to Diana's free hand and was now satisfied that the two people she loved most in the world were safe and happy, disengaged herself and fell back to walk with Marisa, the professor and the dogs.

'Daddy and Diana are going to get married,' she announced, sparkling and triumphant.

'Good for them!' Professor Penrose said. 'There's nothing I like better than a nice wedding.'

'Daddy and Diana and me are going to see my grandpère Moreau next week,' Sofia continued. 'He's French. My Daddy's French too and I'm half French, and Diana's English but she can speak lots of languages.'

'She's a talented lady,' Marisa said.

The three of them walked on for a bit, contented and amicable. Sofia, carefully observing Marisa and Professor Penrose, noticed that they seemed to get on very well and make each other smile. Her mind had begun to hum with conjecture.

'Are you married?' she asked the professor.

'I used to be, but sadly my wife got ill and died two years ago,' he told her.

'Well — you and Marisa could get married, couldn't you?' Sofia said persuasively. 'That would be nice.'

'That's certainly an interesting thought,' said the professor.

'Mmm,' Marisa agreed, looking at him with a wry grin.

Louis and Diana walked on, looking up at the sky. There was just a handful of rose-tinted clouds hovering over the horizon beneath a canopy of clearest blue and luminous gold.

Diana was conscious of a deep sense of joy and fulfilment — and freedom, too; a release from the troubled times earlier in the year when dreams of disaster had dominated her life.

Diana's love had filled Louis with renewed vitality and purpose. The gallery was doing far better than he ever hoped and he had plans for them to buy a small place in France in the coming year.

He was fired with longing to rediscover his homeland — with Diana and Sofia at his side.

'My father will love you,' he told Diana. 'He has a house in Provence at the top of a long, steep track, and in the village there are little cafés where you can sit out as late as midnight in the summer.'

'And the air smells of the countryside and cooking and red wine,' Diana said, loving his surge of new enthusiasm for life.

He hugged her close against him. 'And at night there are pale hunting owls flying over the hills.'

'Heavenly!' she agreed.

Already the sun was sinking towards

the dark line of the horizon. Across the fading brightness of the sky a single magpie dived in a decisive arc, speeding menacingly towards them, veering off at the last minute.

Diana took in a sharp breath.

'Don't you want to look for its mate?' Louis asked, tender and amused.

She smiled and pulled his face down to hers, blocking out every other vision but him.

THE END

APL		CCS	
Cen		Ear	
Mob		Cou	
ALL		Jub	
VAL		CHE	
Ald		Bel	
Fin		Fol	
Can	2-12-13	STO	
TIL		HCL	